Robert Barr (16 September 1849 – 21 October 1912) was a Scottish-Canadian short story writer and novelist. Robert Barr was born in Barony, Lanark, Scotland to Robert Barr and Jane Watson. In 1854, he emigrated with his parents to Upper Canada at the age of four years old. His family settled on a farm near the village of Muirkirk. Barr assisted his father with his job as a carpenter, and developed a sound work ethic. Robert Barr then worked as a steel smelter for a number of years before he was educated at Toronto Normal School in 1873 to train as a teacher. After graduating Toronto Normal School, Barr became a teacher, and eventually headmaster/principal of the Central School of Windsor, Ontario in 1874. While Barr worked as head master of the Central School of Windsor, Ontario, he began to contribute short stories—often based on personal experiences, and recorded his work. On August 1876, when he was 27, Robert Barr married Ontario-born Eva Bennett, who was 21. (Source: Wikipedia)

Literary works:
"The Face And The Mask" (1894)
In the Midst of Alarms (1894, 1900, 1912)
From Whose Bourne (1896)
One Day's Courtship (1896)
Revenge!
The Strong Arm
A Woman Intervenes (1896)
Tekla: A Romance of Love and War (1898)
Jennie Baxter, Journalist (1899)
The Unchanging East (1900)
The Victors (1901)
A Prince of Good Fellows (1902)
Over The Border; A Romance (1903)
The O'Ruddy, A Romance, with Stephen Crane (1903)

ONE DAY'S COURTSHIP
&
FROM WHOSE BOURNE

ROBERT BARR

PRINCE CLASSICS

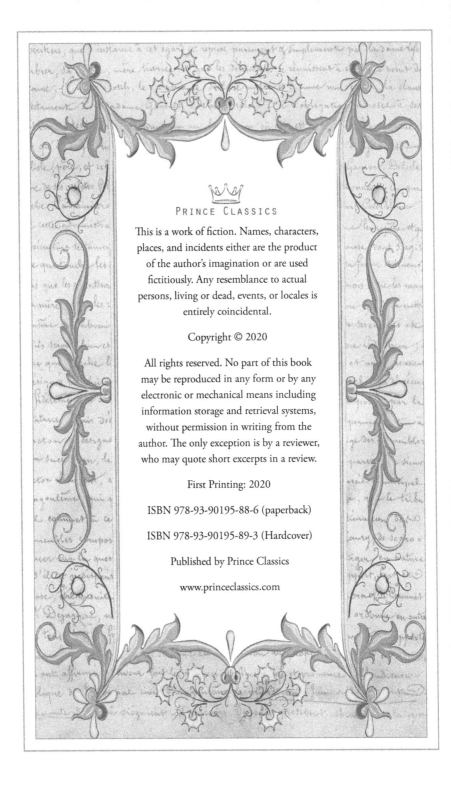

First Printing: 2020

ISBN 978-93-90195-88-6 (paperback)

ISBN 978-93-90195-89-3 (Hardcover)

Published by Prince Classics

www.princeclassics.com

Contents

ONE DAY'S COURTSHIP
&
FROM WHOSE BOURNE

ONE DAY'S COURTSHIP

One Day's Courtship

Chapter I

John Trenton, artist, put the finishing touches to the letter he was writing, and then read it over to himself. It ran as follows:—

"My Dear Ed.,

"I sail for England on the 27th. But before I leave I want to have another look at the Shawenegan Falls. Their roar has been in my ears ever since I left there. That tremendous hillside of foam is before my eyes night and day. The sketches I took are not at all satisfactory, so this time I will bring my camera with me, and try to get some snapshots at the falls.

"Now, what I ask is this. I want you to hold that canoe for me against all comers for Tuesday. Also, those two expert half-breeds. Tell them I am coming, and that there is money in it if they take me up and back as safely as they did before. I don't suppose there will be much demand for the canoe on that day; in fact, it astonishes me that Americans, who appreciate the good things of our country better than we do ourselves, practically know nothing of this superb cataract right at their own doors. I suppose your new canoe is not finished yet, and as the others are up in the woods I write so that you will keep this particular craft for me. I do not wish to take any risks, as I leave so soon. Please drop me a note to this hotel at Quebec, and I will meet you in Le Gres on Tuesday morning at daybreak.

"Your friend,

"John Trenton."

Mason was a millionaire and a lumber king, but every one called him Ed. He owned baronial estates in the pine woods, and saw-mills without number. Trenton had brought a letter of introduction to him from a mutual friend in Quebec, who had urged the artist to visit the Shawenegan Falls. He heard the Englishman inquire about the cataract, and told him that he knew the man who would give him every facility for reaching the falls. Trenton's acquaintance with Mason was about a fortnight old, but already they were the firmest of friends. Any one who appreciated the Shawenegan Falls found a ready path to the heart of the big lumberman. It was almost impossible to reach the falls without the assistance of Mr. Mason. However, he was no monopolist. Any person wishing to visit the cataract got a canoe from the lumber king free of all cost, except a tip to the two boatmen who acted as guides and watermen. The artist had not long to wait for his answer. It was—

"My **Dear John,**

"The canoe is yours; the boatmen are yours: and the Shawenegan is yours for Tuesday. Also,

"I am yours,

"E. Mason."

On Monday evening John Trenton stepped off the C. P. R. train at Three Rivers. With a roughing-it suit on, and his camera slung over his shoulders, no one would have taken him for the successful landscape artist who on Piccadilly was somewhat particular about his attire.

John Trenton was not yet R. A., nor even A. R. A., but all his friends would tell you that, if the Royal Academy was not governed by a clique, he would have been admitted long ago, and that anyhow it was only a question of time. In fact, John admitted this to himself, but to no one else.

He entered the ramshackle 'bus, and was driven a long distance through very sandy streets to the hotel on the St. Lawrence, and, securing a room, made arrangements to be called before daybreak. He engaged the same driver who had taken him out to "The Greys," as it was locally called, on the occasion of his former visit.

The morning was cold and dark. Trenton found the buckboard at the door, and he put his camera under the one seat—a kind of a box for the holding of bits of harness and other odds and ends. As he buttoned up his overcoat he noticed that a great white steamer had come in the night, and was tied up in front of the hotel.

"The Montreal boat," explained the driver.

As they drove along the silent streets of Three Rivers, Trenton called to mind how, on the former occasion, he thought the Lower Canada buckboard by all odds, the most uncomfortable vehicle he had ever ridden in, and he felt that his present experience was going to corroborate this first impression. The seat was set in the centre, between the front and back wheels, on springy boards, and every time the conveyance jolted over a log—a not unfrequent occurrence—the seat went down and the back bent forward, as if to throw him over on the heels of the patient horse.

The road at first was long and straight and sandy, but during the latter part of the ride there were plenty of hills, up many of which a plank roadway ran; so that loads which it would be impossible to take through the deep sand, might be hauled up the steep incline.

At first the houses they passed had a dark and deserted look; then a light twinkled here and there. The early habitant was making his fire. As daylight began gradually to bring out the landscape, the sharp sound of the distant axe was heard. The early habitant was laying in his day's supply of firewood.

"Do you notice how the dawn slowly materialises the landscape?" said the artist to the boy beside him.

The boy saw nothing wonderful about that. Daylight always did it.

"Then it is not unusual in these parts? You see, I am very seldom up at this hour."

The boy wished that was his case.

"Does it not remind you of a photographer in a dark room carefully developing a landscape plate? Not one of those rapid plates, you know, but a slow, deliberate plate."

No, it didn't remind him of anything of the kind. He had never seen either a slow or a rapid plate developed.

"Then you have no prejudices as to which is the best developer, pyrogallic acid or ferrous oxalate, not to mention such recent decoctions as eikonogen, quinol, and others?"

No, the boy had none.

"Well, that's what I like. I like a young man whose mind is open to conviction."

The boy was not a conversational success. He evidently did not enter into the spirit of the artist's remarks. He said most people got off at that point and walked to warm up, and asked Trenton if he would not like to follow their example.

"No, my boy," said the Englishman, "I don't think I shall. You see, I have paid for this ride, and I want to get all I can out of it. I shall shiver here and try to get the worth of my money. But with you it is different. If you want to get down, do so. I will drive."

The boy willingly handed over the reins, and sprang out on the road. Trenton, who was a boy himself that morning, at once whipped up the horse and dashed down the hill to get away from the driver. When a good half-mile had been worried out of the astonished animal, Trenton looked back to see the driver come panting after. The young man was calmly sitting on the back part of the buckboard, and when the horse began to walk again, the boy slid off, and, without a smile on his face, trotted along at the side.

"That fellow has evidently a quiet sense of humour, although he is so careful not to show it," said Trenton to himself.

On reaching the hilltop, they caught a glimpse of the rim of the sun rising gloriously over the treetops on the other side of the St. Maurice River. Trenton stopped the horse, and the boy looked up to see what was wrong. He could not imagine any one stopping merely to look at the sun.

"Isn't that splendid?" cried Trenton, with a deep breath, as he watched the great globe slowly ascend into the sky. The distant branches of the trees were delicately etched against its glowing surface, and seemed to cling to it like tendrils, slipping further and further down as the sun leisurely disentangled itself, and at last stood in its incomparable grandeur full above the forest.

The woods all around had on their marvellous autumn tints, and now the sun added a living lustre to them that made the landscape more brilliant than anything the artist had ever seen before.

"Ye gods!" he cried enthusiastically, "that scene is worth coming from England to have one glimpse of."

"See here," said the driver, "if you want to catch Ed. Mason before he's gone to the woods you'll have to hurry up. It's getting late."

"True, O driver. You have brought me from the sun to the earth. Have you ever heard of the person who fell from the sun to the earth?"

No, he hadn't.

"Well, that was before your time. You will never take such a tumble. I—I suppose they don't worship the sun in these parts?"

No, they didn't.

"When you come to think of it, that is very strange. Have you ever reflected that it is always in warm countries they worship the sun? Now, I should think it ought to be just the other way about. Do you know that when I got on with you this morning I was eighty years old, every day of it. What do you think my age is now?"

"Eighty years, sir."

"Not a bit of it. I'm eighteen. The sun did it. And yet they claim there is no fountain of youth. What fools people are, my boy!"

The young man looked at his fare slyly, and cordially agreed with him.

"You certainly have a concealed sense of humour," said the artist.

They wound down a deep cut in the hill, and got a view of the lumber village—their destination. The roar of the waters tumbling over the granite rocks—the rocks from which the village takes its name—came up the ravine. The broad river swept in a great semicircle to their right, and its dark waters were flecked with the foam of the small falls near the village, and the great cataract miles up the river. It promised to be a perfect autumn day. The sky, which had seemed to Trenton overcast when they started, was now one deep dome of blue without even the suggestion of a cloud.

The buckboard drew up at the gate of the house in which Mr. Mason lived when he was in the lumber village, although his home was at Three Rivers. The old Frenchwoman, Mason's housekeeper, opened the door for Trenton, and he remembered as he went in how the exquisite cleanliness of everything had impressed him during his former visit. She smiled as she recognised the genial Englishman. She had not forgotten his compliments in her own language on her housekeeping some months before, and perhaps she also remembered his liberality. Mr. Mason, she said, had gone to the river to see after the canoe, leaving word that he would return in a few minutes. Trenton, who knew the house, opened the door at his right, to enter the sitting-room and leave there his morning wraps, which the increasing warmth rendered no longer necessary. As he burst into the room in his impetuous way, he was taken aback to see standing at the window, looking out towards the river, a tall young woman. Without changing her position, she looked slowly around at the intruder. Trenton's first thought was a hasty wish that he were better dressed. His roughing-it costume, which up to that time had seemed so comfortable, now appeared uncouth and out of place. He felt as if he had suddenly found himself in a London drawing-room with a shooting-jacket on. But this sensation was quickly effaced by the look which the beauty gave him over her shoulder. Trenton, in all his experience, had never encountered such a glance of indignant scorn. It was a look of resentment and contempt, with just a dash of feminine reproach in it.

"What have I done?" thought the unhappy man; then he stammered aloud, "I—I—really—I beg your pardon. I thought the—ah—room was empty."

The imperious young woman made no reply. She turned to the window again, and Trenton backed out of the room as best he could.

"Well!" he said to himself, as he breathed with relief the outside air again, "that was the rudest thing I ever knew a lady to do. She is a lady, there is no doubt of that. There is nothing of the backwoods about her. But she might at least have answered me. What have I done, I wonder? It must be something terrible and utterly unforgivable, whatever it is. Great heavens!" he murmured, aghast at the thought, "I hope that girl isn't going up to the Shawenegan Falls."

Trenton was no ladies' man. The presence of women always disconcerted him, and made him feel awkward and boorish. He had been too much of a student in higher art to acquire the smaller art of the drawing-room. He felt ill at ease in society, and seemed to have a fatal predilection for saying the wrong thing, and suffered the torture afterwards of remembering what the right thing would have been.

Trenton stood at the gate for a moment, hoping Mason would come. Suddenly he remembered with confusion that he was directly in range of those disdainful eyes in the parlour, and he beat a hasty retreat toward the old mill that stood by the falls. The roar of the turbulent water over the granite rocks had a soothing effect on the soul of the man who knew he was a criminal, yet could not for the life of him tell what his crime had been. Then he wandered up the river-bank toward where he saw the two half-breeds placing the canoe in the still water at the further end of the village. Half-way there he was relieved to meet the genial Ed. Mason, who greeted him, as Trenton thought, with a somewhat overwrought effusion. There evidently was something on the genial Ed.'s mind.

"Hello, old man," he cried, shaking Trenton warmly by the hand. "Been here long? Well, I declare, I'm glad to see you. Going to have a splendid day for it, aren't you? Yes, sir, I am glad to see you."

"When a man says that twice in one breath, a fellow begins to doubt him. Now, you good-natured humbug, what's the matter? What have I done? How did you find me out? Who turned Queen's evidence? Look here, Edward Mason, why are you not glad to see me?"

"Nonsense; you know I am. No one could be more welcome. By the way, my wife's here. You never met her, I think?"

"I saw a young lady remarkably—"

"No, no; that is Miss —. By the way, Trenton, I want you to do me a favour, now that I think of it. Of course the canoe is yours for to-day, but that young woman wants to go up to the Shawenegan. You wouldn't mind her going up with you, would you? You see, I have no other canoe to-day, and she can't stay till to-morrow."

"I shall be delighted, I'm sure," answered Trenton. But he didn't look it.

Chapter II

Eva Sommerton, of Boston, knew that she lived in the right portion of that justly celebrated city, and this knowledge was evident in the poise of her queenly head, and in every movement of her graceful form. Blundering foreigners—foreigners as far as Boston is concerned, although they may be citizens of the United States—considered Boston to be a large city, with commerce and railroads and busy streets and enterprising newspapers, but the true Bostonian knows that this view is very incorrect. The real Boston is penetrated by no railroads. Even the jingle of the street-car bell does not disturb the silence of the streets of this select city. It is to the ordinary Boston what the empty, out-of-season London is to the rest of the busy metropolis. The stranger, jostled by the throng, may not notice that London is empty, but his lordship, if he happens during the deserted period to pass through, knows there is not a soul in town.

Miss Sommerton had many delusions, but fortunately for her peace of mind she had never yet met a candid friend with courage enough to tell her so. It would have required more bravery than the ordinary society person possesses to tell Miss Sommerton about any of her faults. The young gentlemen of her acquaintance claimed that she had no faults, and if her lady friends thought otherwise, they reserved the expression of such opinions for social gatherings not graced by the presence of Miss Sommerton.

Eva Sommerton thought she was not proud, or if there was any tinge of pride in her character, it was pride of the necessary and proper sort.

She also possessed the vain belief that true merit was the one essential, but if true merit had had the misfortune to be presented to Miss Sommerton without an introduction of a strictly unimpeachable nature, there is every reason to fear true merit would not have had the exquisite privilege of basking in the smiles of that young Bostonian. But perhaps her chief delusion was the belief that she was an artist. She had learned all that Boston could teach of drawing, and this thin veneer had received a beautiful foreign polish abroad. Her friends pronounced her sketches really wonderful. Perhaps if Miss Sommerton's entire capital had been something less than her half-yearly income, she might have made a name for herself; but the rich man gets a foretaste of the scriptural difficulty awaiting him at the gates of heaven, when he endeavours to achieve an earthly success, the price of which is hard labour, and not hard cash.

We are told that pride must have a fall, and there came an episode in Miss Sommerton's career as an artist which was a rude shock to her self-complacency. Having purchased a landscape by a celebrated artist whose work she had long admired, she at last ventured to write to him and enclose some of her own sketches, with a request for a candid judgment of them—that is, she said she wanted a candid judgment of them.

The reply seemed to her so ungentlemanly, and so harsh, that, in her vexation and anger, she tore the letter to shreds and stamped her pretty foot with a vehemence which would have shocked those who knew her only as the dignified and self-possessed Miss Eva Sommerton.

Then she looked at her libelled sketches, and somehow they did not appear to be quite so faultless as she had supposed them to be.

This inspection was followed by a thoughtful and tearful period of meditation; and finally, with contriteness, the young woman picked up from her studio floor the shreds of the letter and pasted them carefully together on a white sheet of paper, in which form she still preserved the first honest opinion she had ever received.

In the seclusion of her aesthetic studio Miss Sommerton made a heroic resolve to work hard. Her life was to be consecrated to art. She would win reluctant recognition from the masters. Under all this wave of heroic resolution was an under-current of determination to get even with the artist who had treated her work so contemptuously.

Few of us quite live up to our best intentions, and Miss Sommerton was no exception to the rule. She did not work as devotedly as she had hoped to do, nor did she become a recluse from society. A year after she sent to the artist some sketches which she had taken in Quebec—some unknown waterfalls, some wild river scenery—and received from him a warmer letter of commendation than she had hoped for. He remembered her former sketches, and now saw a great improvement. If the waterfall sketches were not exaggerations, he would like to see the originals. Where were they? The lady was proud of her discoveries in the almost unknown land of Northern Quebec, and she wrote a long letter telling all about them, and a polite note of thanks for the information ended the correspondence.

Miss Sommerton's favourite discovery was that tremendous downward plunge of the St. Maurice, the Falls of Shawenegan. She had sketched it from a dozen different standpoints, and raved about it to her friends, if such a dignified young person as Miss Sommerton could be said to rave over anything. Some Boston people, on her recommendation, had visited the falls, but their account of the journey made so much of the difficulties and discomforts, and so little of the magnificence of the cataract, that our amateur artist resolved to keep the falls, as it were, to herself. She made yearly pilgrimages to the St. Maurice, and came to have a kind of idea of possession which always amused Mr. Mason. She seemed to resent the fact that others went to look at the falls, and, worse than all, took picnic baskets there, actually lunching on its sacred shores, leaving empty champagne bottles and boxes of sardines that had evidently broken some one's favourite knife in the opening. This particular summer she had driven out to "The Greys," but finding that a party was going up in canoes every day that week, she promptly ordered her driver to take her back to Three Rivers, saying to Mr. Mason she would return when she could have the falls to herself.

"You remind me of Miss Porter," said the lumber king.

"Miss Porter! Who is she?"

"When Miss Porter visited England and saw Mr. Gladstone, he asked her if she had ever seen the Niagara Falls. 'Seen them?' she answered. 'Why, I own them!'"

"What did she mean by that? I confess I don't see the point, or perhaps it isn't a joke."

"Oh yes, it is. You mustn't slight my good stories in that way. She meant just what she said. I believe the Porter family own, or did own, Goat Island, and, I suppose, the other bank, and, therefore, the American Fall. The joke—I do dislike to have to explain jokes, especially to you cool, unsympathising Bostonians—is the ridiculousness of any mere human person claiming to own such a thing as the Niagara Falls. I believe, though, that you are quite equal to it—I do indeed."

"Thank you, Mr. Mason."

"I knew you would be grateful when I made myself clearly understood. Now, what I was going to propose is this. You should apply to the Canadian Government for possession of the Shawenegan. I think they would let it go at a reasonable figure. They look on it merely as an annoying impediment to the navigation of the river, and an obstruction which has caused them to spend some thousands of dollars in building a slide by the side of it, so that the logs may come down safely."

"If I owned it, the slide is the first thing I would destroy."

"What? And ruin the lumber industry of the Upper St. Maurice? Oh, you wouldn't do such a thing! If that is your idea, I give you fair warning that I will oppose your claims with all the arts of the lobbyist. If you want to become the private owner of the falls, you should tell the Government that you have some thoughts of encouraging the industries of the province by building a mill—"

"A mill?"

"Yes; why not? Indeed, I have half a notion to put a saw-mill there myself. It always grieves me to see so much magnificent power going to waste."

"Oh, seriously, Mr. Mason, you would never think of committing such an act of sacrilege?"

"Sacrilege, indeed! I like that. Why, the man who makes one saw-mill hum where no mill ever hummed before is a benefactor to his species. Don't they teach political economy at Boston? I thought you liked saw-mills. You drew a very pretty picture of the one down the stream."

"I admire a ruined saw-mill, as that one was; but not one in a state of activity, or of eruption, as a person might say."

"Well, won't you go up to the falls to-day, Miss Sommerton? I assure you we have a most unexceptionable party. Why, one of them is a Government official. Think of that!"

"I refuse to think of it; or, if I do think of it, I refuse to be dazzled by his magnificence. I want to see the Shawenegan, not a picnic party drinking."

"You wrong them, really you do, Miss Sommerton, believe me. You have got your dates mixed. It is the champagne party that goes to-day. The beer crowd is not due until to-morrow."

"The principle is the same."

"The price of the refreshment is not. I speak as a man of bitter experience. Let's see. If recollection holds her throne, I think there was a young lady from New England—I forget the name of the town at the moment—who took a lunch with her the last time she went to the Shawenegan. I merely give this as my impression, you know. I am open to contradiction."

"Certainly, I took a lunch. I always do. I would to-day if I were going up there, and Mrs. Mason would give me some sandwiches. You would give me a lunch, wouldn't you, dear?"

"I'll tell them to get it ready now, if you will only stay," replied that lady, on being appealed to.

"No, it isn't the lunch I object to. I object to people going there merely for the lunch. I go for the scenery; the lunch is incidental."

"When you get the deed of the falls, I'll tell you what we'll do," put in Mason. "We will have a band of trained Indians stationed at the landing, and they will allow no one to disembark who does not express himself in sufficiently ecstatic terms about the great cataract. You will draw up a set of adjectives, which I will give to the Indians, instructing them to allow no one to land who does not use at least three out of five of them in referring to the falls. People whose eloquent appreciation does not reach the required altitude will have to stay there till it does, that's all. We will treat them as we do our juries—starve them into a verdict, and the right verdict at that."

"Don't mind him, Eva. He is just trying to exasperate you. Think of what I have to put up with. He goes on like that all the time," said Mrs. Mason.

"Really, my dear, your flattery confuses me. You can't persuade any one that I keep up this brilliancy in the privacy of my own house. It is only turned on for company."

"Why, Mr. Mason, I didn't think you looked on me as company. I thought I enjoyed the friendship of the Mason family."

"Oh, you do, you do indeed! The company I referred to was the official party which has just gone to the falls. This is some of the brilliancy left over. But, really, you had better stay after coming all this distance."

"Yes, do, Eva. Let me go back with you to the Three Rivers, and then you stay with me till next week, when you can visit the falls all alone. It is very pleasant at Three Rivers just now. And besides, we can go for a day's shopping at Montreal."

"I wish I could."

"Why, of course you can," said Mason. "Imagine the delight of smuggling your purchases back to Boston. Confess that this is a pleasure you hadn't thought of."

"I admit the fascination of it all, but you see I am with a party that has gone on to Quebec, and I just got away for a day. I am to meet them there to-night or to-morrow morning. But I will return in the autumn, Mrs. Mason, when it is too late for the picnics. Then, Mr. Mason, take warning. I mean to have a canoe to myself, or—well, you know the way we Bostonians treated you Britishers once upon a time."

"Distinctly. But we will return good for evil, and give you warm tea instead of the cold mixture you so foolishly brewed in the harbour."

As the buckboard disappeared around the corner, and Mr. and Mrs. Mason walked back to the house, the lady said—

"What a strange girl Eva is."

"Very. Don't she strike you as being a trifle selfish?"

"Selfish? Eva Sommerton? Why, what could make you think such a thing? What an absurd idea! You cannot imagine how kind she was to me when I visited Boston."

"Who could help it, my dear? I would have been so myself if I had happened to meet you there."

"Now, Ed., don't be absurd."

"There is something absurd in being kind to a person's wife, isn't there? Well, it struck me her objection to any one else being at the falls, when her ladyship was there, might seem—not to me, of course, but to an outsider—a trifle selfish."

"Oh, you don't understand her at all. She has an artistic temperament, and she is quite right in wishing to be alone. Now, Ed., when she does come again I want you to keep anyone else from going up there. Don't forget it, as you do most of the things I tell you. Say to anybody who wants to go up that the canoes are out of repair."

"Oh, I can't say that, you know. Anything this side of a crime I am willing to commit; but to perjure myself, no, not for Venice. Can you think of any other method that will combine duplicity with a clear conscience? I'll tell you what I'll do. I will have the canoe drawn up, and gently, but firmly, slit it with my knife. One of the men can mend it in ten minutes. Then I can look even the official from Quebec in the face, and tell him truly that the canoe will not hold water. I suppose as long as my story will hold water you and Miss Sommerton will not mind?"

"If the canoe is ready for her when she comes, I shall be satisfied. Please to remember I am going to spend a week or two in Boston next winter."

"Oh ho, that's it, is it? Then it was not pure philanthropy—"

"Pure nonsense, Ed. I want the canoe to be ready, that's all."

When Mrs. Mason received the letter from Miss Sommerton, stating the time the young woman intended to pay her visit to the Shawenegan, she gave the letter to her husband, and reminded him of the necessity of keeping the canoe for that particular date. As the particular date was some weeks off, and as Ed. Mason was a man who never crossed a stream until he came to it, he said, "All right," put the letter in his inside pocket, and the next time he thought of it was on the fine autumn afternoon—Monday afternoon—when he saw Mrs. Mason drive up to the door of his lumber-woods residence with Miss Eva Sommerton in the buggy beside her. The young lady wondered, as Mr. Mason helped her out, if that genial gentleman, whom she regarded as the most fortunate of men, had in reality some secret, gnawing sorrow the world knew not of.

"Why, Ed., you look ill," exclaimed Mrs. Mason; "is there anything the matter?"

"Oh, it is nothing—at least, not of much consequence. A little business worry, that's all."

"Has there been any trouble?"

"Oh no—at the least, not yet."

"Trouble about the men, is it?"

"No, not about the men," said the unfortunate gentleman, with a somewhat unnecessary emphasis on the last word.

"Oh, Mr. Mason, I am afraid I have come at a wrong time. If so, don't hesitate to tell me. If I can do anything to help you, I hope I may be allowed."

"You have come just at the right time," said the lumberman, "and you are very welcome, I assure you. If I find I need help, as perhaps I may, you will be reminded of your promise."

To put off as long as possible the evil time of meeting his wife, Mason went with the man to see the horse put away, and he lingered an unnecessarily long time in ascertaining that everything was right in the stable. The man was astonished to find his master so particular that afternoon. A crisis may be postponed, but it can rarely be avoided altogether, and knowing he had to face the inevitable sooner or later, the unhappy man, with a sigh, betook himself to the house, where he found his wife impatiently waiting for him. She closed the door and confronted him.

"Now, Ed., what's the matter?"

"Where's Miss Sommerton?" was the somewhat irrelevant reply.

"She has gone to her room. Ed., don't keep me in suspense. What is wrong?"

"You remember John Trenton, who was here in the summer?"

"I remember hearing you speak of him. I didn't meet him, you know."

"Oh, that's so. Neither you did. You see, he's an awful good fellow, Trenton is—that is, for an Englishman."

"Well, what has Trenton to do with the trouble?"

"Everything, my dear—everything."

"I see how it is. Trenton visited the Shawenegan?"

"He did."

"And he wants to go there again?"

"He does."

"And you have gone and promised him the canoe for to-morrow?"

"The intuition of woman, my dear, is the most wonderful thing on earth."

"It is not half so wonderful as the negligence of man—I won't say the stupidity."

"Thank you, Jennie, for not saying it, but I really think I would feel better if you did."

"Now, what are you going to do about it?"

"Well, my dear, strange as it may appear, that very question has been racking my brain for the last ten minutes. Now, what would you do in my position?"

"Oh, I couldn't be in your position."

"No, that's so, Jennie. Excuse me for suggesting the possibility. I really think this trouble has affected my mind a little. But if you had a husband—if a sensible woman like you could have a husband who got himself into such a position—what would you advise him to do?"

"Now, Ed., don't joke. It's too serious."

"My dear, no one on earth can have such a realisation of its seriousness as I have at this moment. I feel as Mark Twain did with that novel he never finished. I have brought things to a point where I can't go any further. The game seems blocked. I wonder if Miss Sommerton would accept ten thousand feet of lumber f.o.b. and call it square."

"Really, Ed., if you can't talk sensibly, I have nothing further to say."

"Well, as I said, the strain is getting too much for me. Now, don't go away, Jennie. Here is what I am thinking of doing. I'll speak to Trenton. He won't mind Miss Sommerton's going in the canoe with him. In fact, I should think he would rather like it."

"Dear me, Ed., is that all the progress you've made? I am not troubling myself about Mr. Trenton. The difficulty will be with Eva. Do you think for a moment she will go if she imagined herself under obligations to a stranger for the canoe? Can't you get Mr. Trenton to put off his visit until the day after tomorrow? It isn't long to wait."

"No, that is impossible. You see, he has just time to catch his steamer as it is. No, he has the promise in writing, while Miss Sommerton has no legal evidence if this thing ever gets into the courts. Trenton has my written promise. You see, I did not remember the two dates were the same. When I wrote to Trenton—"

"Ed., don't try to excuse yourself. You had her letter in your pocket, you know you had. This is a matter for which there is no excuse, and it cannot be explained away."

"That's so, Jennie. I am down in the depths once more. I shall not try to crawl out again—at least, not while my wife is looking."

"No, your plan will not work. I don't know that any will. There is only one thing to try, and it is this—Miss Sommerton must think that the canoe is hers. You must appeal to her generosity to let Mr. Trenton go with her."

"Won't you make the appeal, Jen?"

"No, I will not. In the first place she'll be sorry for you, because you will make such a bungle of it. Trial is your only hope."

"Oh, if success lies in bungling, I will succeed."

"Don't be too sure. I suppose that man will be here by daybreak to-morrow?"

"Not so bad as that, Jennie. You always try to put the worst face on things. He won't be here till sunrise at the earliest."

"I will ask Eva to come down."

"You needn't hurry just because of me. Besides, I would like a few moments to prepare myself for my fate. Even a murderer is given a little time."

"Not a moment, Ed. We had better get this thing settled as soon as possible."

"Perhaps you are right," he murmured, with a deep sigh. "Well, if we Britishers, as Miss S. calls us, ever faced the Americans with as faint a heart as I do now, I don't wonder we got licked."

"Don't say 'licked,' Ed."

"I believe it's historical. Oh, I see. You object to the word, not to the allegation. Well, I won't cavil about that. All my sympathy just now is concentrated on one unfortunate Britisher. My dear, let the sacrifice begin."

Mrs. Mason went to the stairway and called—

"Eva, dear, can you come down for a moment? We want you to help us out of a difficulty."

Miss Sommerton appeared smilingly, smoothing down the front of the dress that had taken the place of the one she travelled in. She advanced towards Mason with sweet compassion in her eyes, and that ill-fated man thought he had never seen any one look so altogether charming—excepting, of course, his own wife in her youthful days. She seemed to have smoothed away all the Boston stiffness as she smoothed her dress.

"Oh, Mr. Mason," she said, sympathetically, as she approached, "I am so sorry anything has happened to trouble you, and I do hope I am not intruding."

"Indeed, you are not, Miss Eva. In fact, your sympathy has taken away half the trouble already, and I want to beg of you to help me off with the other half."

A glance at his wife's face showed him that he had not made a bad beginning.

"Miss Sommerton, you said you would like to kelp me. Now I am going to appeal to you. I throw myself on your mercy."

There was a slight frown on Mrs. Mason's face, and her husband felt that he was perhaps appealing too much.

"In fact, the truth is, my wife gave me—"

Here a cough interrupted him, and he paused and ran his hand through his hair. "Pray don't mind me, Mr. Mason," said Miss Sommerton, "if you would rather not tell—"

"Oh, but I must; that is, I want you to know."

He glanced at his wife, but there was no help there, so he plunged in headlong.

"To tell the truth, there is a friend of mine who wants to go to the falls to-morrow. He sails for Europe immediately, and has no other day."

The Boston rigidity perceptibly returned.

"Oh, if that is all, you needn't have had a moment's trouble. I can just as well put off my visit."

"Oh, can you?" cried Mason, joyously.

His wife sat down in the rocking-chair with a sigh of despair. Her infatuated husband thought he was getting along famously.

"Then your friends are not waiting for you at Quebec this time, and you can stay a day or two with us."

"Eva's friends are at Montreal, Edward, and she cannot stay."

"Oh, then—why, then, to-morrow's your only day, too?"

"It doesn't matter in the least, Mr. Mason. I shall be most glad to put off my visit to oblige your friend—no, I didn't mean that," she cried, seeing the look of anguish on Mason's face, "it is to oblige you. Now, am I not good?"

"No, you are cruel," replied Mason. "You are going up to the falls. I insist on that. Let's take that as settled. The canoe is yours." He caught an encouraging look from his wife. "If you want to torture me you will say you will not go. If you want to do me the greatest of favours, you will let my friend go in the canoe with you to the landing."

"What! go alone with a stranger?" cried Miss Sommerton, freezingly.

"No, the Indians will be there, you know."

"Oh, I didn't expect to paddle the canoe myself."

"I don't know about that. You strike me as a girl who would paddle her own canoe pretty well."

"Now, Edward," said his wife. "He wants to take some photographs of the falls, and—"

"Photographs? Why, Ed., I thought you said he was an artist."

"Isn't a photographer an artist?"

"You know he isn't."

"Well, my dear, you know they put on their signs, 'artist—photographer, pictures taken in cloudy weather.' But he's an amateur photographer; an amateur is not so bad as a professional, is he, Miss Sommerton?"

"I think he's worse, if there is any choice. A professional at least takes good pictures, such as they are."

"He is an elderly gentleman, and I am sure—"

"Oh, is he?" cried Miss Sommerton; "then the matter is settled. He shall go. I thought it was some young fop of an amateur photographer."

"Oh, quite elderly. His hair is grey, or badly tinged at least."

The frown on Miss Sommerton's brow cleared away, and she smiled in a manner that was cheering to the heart of her suppliant. He thought it reminded him of the sun breaking through the clouds over the hills beyond the St. Maurice.

"Why, Mr. Mason, how selfishly I've been acting, haven't I? You really must forgive me. It is so funny, too, making you beg for a seat in your own canoe."

"Oh no, it's your canoe—that is, after twelve o'clock to-night. That's when your contract begins."

"The arrangement does not seem to me quite regular; but, then, this is the Canadian woods, and not Boston. But, I want to make my little proviso. I do not wish to be introduced to this man; he must have no excuse for beginning a conversation with me. I don't want to talk to-morrow."

"Heroic resolution," murmured Mason.

32

"So, I do not wish to see the gentleman until I go into the canoe. You can be conveniently absent. Mrs. Perrault will take me down there; she speaks no English, and it is not likely he can speak French."

"We can arrange that."

"Then it is settled, and all I hope for is a good day to-morrow."

Mrs. Mason sprang up and kissed the fair Bostonian, and Mason felt a sensation of joyous freedom that recalled his youthful days when a half-holiday was announced.

"Oh, it is too good of you," said the elder lady.

"Not a bit of it," whispered Miss Sommerton; "I hate the man before I have seen him."

Chapter III

When John Trenton came in to breakfast, he found his friend Mason waiting for him. That genial gentleman was evidently ill at ease, but he said in an offhand way—

"The ladies have already breakfasted. They are busily engaged in the preparations for the trip, and so you and I can have a snack together, and then we will go and see to the canoe."

After breakfast they went together to the river, and found the canoe and the two half-breeds waiting for them. A couple of rugs were spread on the bottom of the canoe rising over the two slanting boards which served as backs to the lowly seats.

"Now," said Mason with a blush, for he always told a necessary lie with some compunction, "I shall have to go and see to one of my men who was injured in the mill this morning. You had better take your place in the canoe, and wait for your passenger, who, as is usual with ladies, will probably be a little late. I think you should sit in the back seat, as you are the heavier of the two. I presume you remember what I told you about sitting in a canoe? Get in with caution while these two men hold the side of it; sit down carefully, and keep steady, no matter what happens. Perhaps you may as well put your camera here at the back, or in the prow."

"No," said Trenton, "I shall keep it slung over my shoulder. It isn't heavy, and I am always afraid of forgetting it if I leave it anywhere."

Trenton got cautiously into the canoe, while Mason bustled off with a very guilty feeling at his heart. He never thought of blaming Miss Sommerton for the course she had taken, and the dilemma into which she placed him, for he felt that the fault was entirely his own.

John Trenton pulled out his pipe, and, absent-mindedly, stuffed it full of tobacco. Just as he was about to light it, he remembered there was to be a lady in the party, and so with a grimace of disappointment he put the loaded pipe into his pocket again.

It was the most lovely time of the year. The sun was still warm, but the dreaded black fly and other insect pests of the region had disappeared before the sharp frosts that occurred every night. The hilly banks of the St. Maurice were covered with unbroken forest, and "the woods of autumn all around, the vale had put their glory on." Presently Trenton saw Miss Sommerton, accompanied by old Mrs. Perrault, coming over the brow of the hill. He attempted to rise, in order to assist the lady to a seat in the canoe, when the half-breed-said in French—:

"Better sit still. It is safer. We will help the lady."

Miss Sommerton was talking rapidly in French—with rather overdone eagerness—to Mrs. Perrault. She took no notice of her fellow-voyager as she lightly stepped exactly in the centre of the canoe, and sank down on the rug in front of him, with the ease of one thoroughly accustomed to that somewhat treacherous craft. The two stalwart boatmen—one at the prow, the other at the stern of the canoe—with swift and dexterous strokes, shot it out into the stream. Trenton could not but admire the knowledge of these two men and their dexterous use of it. Here they were on a swiftly flowing river, with a small fall behind them and a tremendous cataract several miles in front, yet these two men, by their knowledge of the currents, managed to work their way up stream with the least possible amount of physical exertion. The St. Maurice at this point is about half a mile wide, with an island here and there, and now and then a touch of rapids. Sometimes the men would dash right across the river to the opposite bank, and there fall in with a miniature Gulf Stream that would carry them onward without exertion. Sometimes they were near the densely wooded shore, sometimes in the center of the river. The half-breed who stood behind Trenton, leant over to him, and whispered—

"You can now smoke if you like, the wind is down stream."

Naturally, Mr. Trenton wished to smoke. The requesting of permission to do so, it struck him, might open the way to conversation. He was not an ardent conversationalist, but it seemed to him rather ridiculous that two persons should thus travel together in a canoe without saying a word to each other.

"I beg your pardon, madam," he began; "but would you have any objection to my smoking? I am ashamed to confess that I am a slave to the pernicious habit."

There was a moment or two of silence, broken only by the regular dip of the paddle, then Miss Sommerton said, "If you wish to desecrate this lovely spot by smoking, I presume anything I can say will not prevent you."

Trenton was amazed at the rudeness of this reply, and his face flushed with anger. Finally he said, "You must have a very poor opinion of me!"

Miss Sommerton answered tartly, "I have no opinion whatever of you." Then, with womanly inconsistency, she proceeded to deliver her opinion, saying, "A man who would smoke here would smoke in a cathedral."

"I think you are wrong there," said Mr. Trenton, calmly. "I would smoke here, but I would not think of smoking in a cathedral. Neither would I smoke in the humblest log-cabin chapel."

"Sir," said Miss Sommerton, turning partly round, "I came to the St. Maurice for the purpose of viewing its scenery. I hoped to see it alone. I have been disappointed in that, but I must insist on seeing it in silence. I do not wish to carry on a conversation, nor do I wish to enter into a discussion on any subject whatever. I am sorry to have to say this, but it seems to be necessary."

Her remarks so astonished Trenton that he found it impossible to get angrier than he had been when she first spoke. In fact, he found his anger receding rather than augmenting. It was something so entirely new to meet a lady who had such an utter disregard for the rules of politeness that obtain in any civilized society that Mr. Trenton felt he was having a unique and valuable experience.

"Will you pardon me," he said, with apparent submissiveness—"will you pardon me if I disregard your request sufficiently to humbly beg forgiveness for having spoken to you in the first place?"

To this Miss Sommerton made no reply, and the canoe glided along.

After going up the river for a few miles the boatmen came to a difficult part of the voyage. Here the river was divided by an island. The dark waters moved with great swiftness, and with the smoothness of oil, over the concealed rocks, breaking into foam at the foot of the rapids. Now for the first time the Indians had hard work. For quite half an hour they paddled as if in despair, and the canoe moved upward inch by inch. It was not only hard work, but it was work that did not allow of a moment's rest until it was finished. Should the paddles pause but an instant, the canoe would be swept to the bottom of the rapids. When at last the craft floated into the still water above the rapids, the boatmen rested and mopped the perspiration from their brows. Then, without a word, they resumed their steady, easy swing of the paddle. In a short time the canoe drew up at a landing, from which a path ascended the steep hill among the trees. The silence was broken only by the deep, distant, low roar of the Shawenegan Falls. Mr. Trenton sat in his place, while the half-breeds held the canoe steady. Miss Sommerton rose and stepped with firm, self-reliant tread on the landing. Without looking backward she proceeded up the steep hill, and disappeared among the dense foliage. Then Trenton leisurely got out of the canoe.

"You had a hard time of it up that rapid," said the artist in French to the boatmen. "Here is a five-dollar bill to divide when you get down; and, if you bring us safely back, I shall have another ready for you."

The men were profusely grateful, as indeed they had a right to be, for the most they expected was a dollar each as a fee.

"Ah," said the elder, "if we had gentlemen like you to take up every day," and he gave an expressive shrug.

"You shouldn't take such a sordid view of the matter," said the artist. "I should think you would find great pleasure in taking up parties of handsome ladies such as I understand now and then visit the falls."

"Ah," said the boatman, "it is very nice, of course; but, except from Miss Sommerton, we don't get much."

"Really," said the artist; "and who is Miss Sommerton, pray?"

The half-breed nodded up the path.

"Oh, indeed, that is her name. I did not know."

"Yes," said the man, "she is very generous, and she always brings us tobacco in her pocket—good tobacco."

"Tobacco!" cried the artist. "The arrant hypocrite. She gives you tobacco, does she? Did you understand what we were talking about coming up here?"

The younger half-breed was about to say "Yes," and a gleam of intelligence came into his face; but a frown on the other's brow checked him, and the elder gravely shook his head.

"We do not understand English," he said.

As Trenton walked slowly up the steep hillside, he said to himself, "That young woman does not seem to have the slightest spark of gratitude in her composition. Here I have been good-natured enough to share my canoe with her, yet she treats me as if I were some low ruffian instead of a gentleman."

As Miss Sommerton was approaching the Shawenegan Falls, she said to herself, "What an insufferable cad that man is? Mr. Mason doubtless told him that he was indebted to me for being allowed to come in the canoe, and yet, although he must see I do not wish to talk with him, he tried to force conversation on me."

Miss Sommerton walked rapidly along the very imperfect woodland path, which was completely shaded by the overhanging trees. After a walk of nearly a mile, the path suddenly ended at the top of a tremendous precipice of granite, and opposite this point the great hillside of tumbling white foam plunged for ever downward. At the foot of the falls the waters flung themselves against the massive granite barrier, and then, turning at a right angle, plunged downward in a series of wild rapids that completely eclipsed in picturesqueness and grandeur and force even the famous rapids at Niagara. Contemplating this incomparable scene, Miss Sommerton forgot all about her objectionable travelling companion. She sat down on a fallen log, placing her sketch-book on her lap, but it lay there idly as, unconscious of the passing time, she gazed dreamily at the great falls and listened to their vibrating deafening roar. Suddenly the consciousness of some one near startled her from her reverie. She sprang to her feet, and had so completely forgotten her companion that she stared at him for a moment in dumb amazement. He stood back some distance from her, and beside him on its slender tripod was placed a natty little camera. Connected with the instantaneous shutter was a long black rubber tube almost as thin as a string. The bulb of this instantaneous attachment Mr. Trenton held in his hand, and the instant Miss Sommerton turned around, the little shutter, as if in defiance of her, gave a snap, and she knew her picture had been taken, and also that she was the principal object in the foreground.

"You have photographed me, sir!" cried the young woman, with her eyes blazing.

"I have photographed the falls, or, at least, I hope I have," replied Trenton.

"But my picture is in the foreground. You must destroy that plate."

"You will excuse me, Miss Sommerton, if I tell you I shall do nothing of the kind. It is very unusual with me to deny the request of a lady, but in this case I must do so. This is the last plate I have, and it may be the one successful picture of the lot. I shall, therefore, not destroy the plate."

"Then, sir, you are not a gentleman!" cried the impetuous young lady, her face aflame with anger.

"I never claimed to be one," answered Trenton, calmly.

"I shall appeal to Mr. Mason; perhaps he has some means of making you understand that you are not allowed to take a lady's photograph without her permission, and in defiance of her wishes."

"Will you allow me to explain why it is unnecessary to destroy the plate? If you understand anything about photography, you must be aware of the fact—"

"I am happy to say I know nothing of photography, and I desire to know nothing of it. I will not hear any explanation from you, sir. You have refused to destroy the plate. That is enough for me. Your conduct to-day has been entirely contemptible. In the first place you have forced yourself, through Mr. Mason, into my company. The canoe was mine for to-day, and you knew it. I granted you permission to come, but I made it a proviso that there should be no conversation. Now, I shall return in the canoe alone, and I shall pay the boatmen to come back for you this evening." With this she swept indignantly past Mr. Trenton, leaving the unfortunate man for the second or third time that day too much dumbfounded to reply. She marched down the path toward the landing. Arriving at the canoe, she told the boatmen they would have to return for Mr. Trenton; that she was going back alone, and she would pay them handsomely for their extra trip. Even the additional pay offered did not seem to quite satisfy the two half-breeds.

"It will be nearly dark before we can get back," grumbled the elder boatman.

"That does not matter," replied Miss Sommerton, shortly.

"But it is dangerous going down the river at night."

"That does not matter," was again the reply.

"But he has nothing—"

"The longer you stand talking here the longer it will be before you get back. If you are afraid for the safety of the gentleman, pray stay here with him and give me the paddle—I will take the boat down alone."

The boatman said nothing more, but shot the canoe out from the landing and proceeded rapidly down the stream.

Miss Sommerton meditated bitterly on the disappointments and annoyances of the day. Once fairly away, conscience began to trouble her, and she remembered that the gentleman so unceremoniously left in the woods without any possibility of getting away was a man whom Mr. Mason, her friend, evidently desired very much to please. Little had been said by the boatmen, merely a brief word of command now and then from the elder who stood in the stern, until they passed down the rapids. Then Miss Sommerton caught a grumbling word in French which made her heart stand still.

"What is that you said?" she cried to the elder boatman.

He did not answer, but solemnly paddled onward.

"Answer me," demanded Miss Sommerton. "What is that you said about the gentleman who went up with us this morning?"

"I said," replied the half-breed, with a grim severity that even the remembrance of gifts of tobacco could not mitigate, "that the canoe belonged to him today."

"How dare you say such a thing! The canoe was mine. Mr. Mason gave it to me. It was mine for to-day."

"I know nothing about that," returned the boatman doggedly; "but I do know that three days ago Mr. Mason came to me with this gentleman's letter in his hand and said, 'Pierre, Mr. Trenton is to have the canoe for Tuesday. See it is in good order, and no one else is to have it for that day.' That is what Mr. Mason said, and when they were down at the canoe this morning, Mr. Mason asked Mr. Trenton if he would let you go up to the falls in his canoe, and he said 'Yes.'"

Miss Sommerton sat there too horrified to speak. A wild resentment against the duplicity of Ed. Mason arose for a moment in her heart, but it speedily sank as she viewed her own conduct in the light of this astounding revelation. She had abused an unknown gentleman like a pickpocket, and had finally gone off with his canoe, leaving him marooned, as it were, to whose courtesy she was indebted for being there at all. Overcome by the thoughts that crowded so quickly upon her, she buried her face in her hands and wept. But this was only for an instant. Raising her head again, with the imperious air characteristic of her, she said to the boatman—

"Turn back at once, please."

"We are almost there now," he answered, amazed at the feminine inconsistency of the command.

"Turn back at once, I say. You are not too tired to paddle up the river again, are you?"

"No, madame," he answered, "but it is so useless; we are almost there. We shall land you, and then the canoe will go up lighter."

"I wish to go with you. Do what I tell you, and I will pay you."

The stolid boatman gave the command; the man at the bow paddled one way, while the man at the stern paddled another, and the canoe swung round upstream again.

Chapter IV

The sun had gone down when Miss Sommerton put her foot once more on the landing.

"We will go and search for him," said the boatman.

"Stay where you are," she commanded, and disappeared swiftly up the path. Expecting to find him still at the falls, she faced the prospect of a good mile of rough walking in the gathering darkness without flinching. But at the brow of the hill, within hearing distance of the landing, she found the man of whom she was in search. In her agony of mind Miss Sommerton had expected to come upon him pacing moodily up and down before the falls, meditating on the ingratitude of womankind. She discovered him in a much less romantic attitude. He was lying at full length below a white birch-tree, with his camera-box under his head for a pillow. It was evident he had seen enough of the Shawenegan Falls for one day, and doubtless, because of the morning's early rising, and the day's long journey, had fallen soundly asleep. His soft felt hat lay on the ground beside him. Miss Sommerton looked at him for a moment, and thought bitterly of Mason's additional perjury in swearing that he was an elderly man. True, his hair was tinged with grey at the temples, but there was nothing elderly about his appearance. Miss Sommerton saw that he was a handsome man, and wondered this had escaped her notice before, forgetting that she had scarcely deigned to look at him. She thought he had spoken to her with inexcusable bluntness at the falls, in refusing to destroy his plate; but she now remembered with compunction that he had made no allusion to his ownership of the boat for that day, while she had boasted that it was hers. She determined to return and send one of the boatmen up to awaken him, but at that moment Trenton suddenly opened his eyes, as a person often does when some one looks at him in his sleep. He sprang quickly to his feet, and put up his hand in bewilderment to remove his hat, but found it wasn't there. Then he laughed uncomfortably, stooping to pick it up again.

"I—I—I wasn't expecting visitors," he stammered—

"Why did you not tell me," she said, "that Mr. Mason had promised you the boat for the day?"

"Good gracious!" cried Trenton, "has Ed. Mason told you that?"

"I have not seen Mr. Mason," she replied; "I found it out by catching an accidental remark made by one of the boatmen. I desire very humbly to apologise to you for my conduct."

"Oh, that doesn't matter at all, I assure you."

"What! My conduct doesn't?"

"No, I didn't mean quite that; but I—Of course, you did treat me rather abruptly; but then, you know, I saw how it was. You looked on me as an interloper, as it were, and I think you were quite justified, you know, in speaking as you did. I am a very poor hand at conversing with ladies, even at my best, and I am not at my best to-day. I had to get up too early, so there is no doubt what I said was said very awkwardly indeed. But it really doesn't matter, you know—that is, it doesn't matter about anything you said."

"I think it matters very much—at least, it matters very much to me. I shall always regret having treated you as I did, and I hope you will forgive me for having done so."

"Oh, that's all right," said Mr. Trenton, swinging his camera over his shoulder. "It is getting dark, Miss Sommerton; I think we should hurry down to the canoe."

As they walked down the hill together, he continued—

"I wish you would let me give you a little lesson in photography, if you don't mind."

"I have very little interest in photography, especially amateur photography," replied Miss Sommerton, with a partial return of her old reserve.

"Oh, I don't wish to make an amateur photographer of you. You sketch very nicely, and—"

44

"How do you know that?" asked Miss Sommerton, turning quickly towards him: "you have never seen any of my sketches."

"Ah, well," stammered Trenton, "no—that is—you know—are not those water-colours in Mason's house yours?"

"Mr. Mason has some of my sketches. I didn't know you had seen them."

"Well, as I was saying," continued Trenton, "I have no desire to convert you to the beauties of amateur photography. I admit the results in many cases are very bad. I am afraid if you saw the pictures I take myself you would not be much in love with the art. But what I wish to say is in mitigation of my refusal to destroy the plate when you asked me to."

"Oh, I beg you will not mention that, or refer to anything at all I have said to you. I assure you it pains me very much, and you know I have apologised once or twice already."

"Oh, it isn't that. The apology should come from me; but I thought I would like to explain why it is that I did not take your picture, as you thought I did."

"Not take my picture? Why I saw you take it. You admitted yourself you took it."

"Well, you see, that is what I want to explain. I took your picture, and then again I didn't take it. This is how it is with amateur photography. Your picture on the plate will be a mere shadow, a dim outline, nothing more. No one can tell who it is. You see, it is utterly impossible to take a dark object and one in pure white at the instantaneous snap. If the picture of the falls is at all correct, as I expect it will be, then your picture will be nothing but a shadow unrecognisable by any one."

"But they do take pictures with the cataract as a background, do they not? I am sure I have seen photos of groups taken at Niagara Falls; in fact, I have seen groups being posed in public for that purpose, and very silly they looked, I must say. I presume that is one of the things that has prejudiced me so much against the camera."

"Those pictures, Miss Sommerton, are not genuine; they are not at all what they pretend to be. The prints that you have seen are the results of the manipulation of two separate plates, one of the plates containing the group or the person photographed, and the other an instantaneous picture of the falls. If you look closely at one of those pictures you will see a little halo of light or dark around the person photographed. That, to an experienced photographer, shows the double printing. In fact, it is double dealing all round. The deluded victim of the camera imagines that the pictures he gets of the falls, with himself in the foreground, is really a picture of the falls taken at the time he is being photographed. Whereas, in the picture actually taken of him, the falls themselves are hopelessly over-exposed, and do not appear at all on the plate. So with the instantaneous picture I took; there will really be nothing of you on that plate that you would recognise as yourself. That was why I refused to destroy it."

"I am afraid," said Miss Sommerton, sadly, "you are trying to make my punishment harder and harder. I believe in reality you are very cruel. You know how badly I feel about the whole matter, and now even the one little point that apparently gave me any excuse is taken away by your scientific explanation."

"Candidly, Miss Sommerton, I am more of a culprit than you imagine, and I suppose it is the tortures of a guilty conscience that caused me to make this explanation. I shall now confess without reserve. As you sat there with your head in your hand looking at the falls, I deliberately and with malice aforethought took a timed picture, which, if developed, will reveal you exactly as you sat, and which will not show the falls at all."

Miss Sommerton walked in silence beside him, and he could not tell just how angry she might be. Finally he said, "I shall destroy that plate, if you order me to."

Miss Sommerton made no reply, until they were nearly at the canoe. Then she looked up at him with a smile, and said, "I think it a pity to destroy any pictures you have had such trouble to obtain."

"Thank you, Miss Sommerton," said the artist. He helped her into the canoe in the gathering dusk, and then sat down himself. But neither of them saw the look of anxiety on the face of the elder boatman. He knew the River St. Maurice.

Chapter V

From the words the elder boatman rapidly addressed to the younger, it was evident to Mr. Trenton that the half-breed was anxious to pass the rapids before it became very much darker.

The landing is at the edge of comparatively still water. At the bottom of the falls the river turns an acute angle and flows to the west. At the landing it turns with equal abruptness, and flows south.

The short westward section of the river from the falls to the point where they landed is a wild, turbulent rapid, in which no boat can live for a moment. From the Point downwards, although the water is covered with foam, only one dangerous place has to be passed. Toward that spot the stalwart half-breeds bent all their energy in forcing the canoe down with the current. The canoe shot over the darkening rapid with the speed of an arrow. If but one or two persons had been in it, the chances are the passage would have been made in safety. As it was one wrong turn of the paddle by the younger half-breed did the mischief. The bottom barely touched a sharp-pointed hidden rock, and in an instant the canoe was slit open as with a knife.

As he sat there Trenton felt the cold water rise around him with a quickness that prevented his doing anything, even if he had known what to do.

"Sit still!" cried the elder boatman; and then to the younger he shouted sharply, "The shore!"

They were almost under the hanging trees when the four found themselves in the water. Trenton grasped an overhanging branch with one hand, and with the other caught Miss Sommerton by the arm. For a moment it was doubtful whether the branch would hold. The current was very swift, and it threw each of them against the rock bank, and bent the branch down into the water.

"Catch hold of me!" cried Trenton. "Catch hold of my coat; I need both hands."

Miss Sommerton, who had acted with commendable bravery throughout, did as she was directed. Trenton, with his released hand, worked himself slowly up the branch, hand over hand, and finally catching a sapling that grew close to the water's edge, with a firm hold, reached down and helped Miss Sommerton on the bank. Then he slowly drew himself up to a safe position and looked around for any signs of the boatmen. He shouted loudly, but there was no answer.

"Are they drowned, do you think?" asked Miss Sommerton, anxiously.

"No, I don't suppose they are; I don't think you could drown a half-breed. They have done their best to drown us, and as we have escaped I see no reason why they should drown."

"Oh, it's all my fault! all my fault!" wailed Miss Sommerton.

"It is, indeed," answered Trenton, briefly.

She tried to straighten herself up, but, too wet and chilled and limp to be heroic, she sank on a rock and began to cry.

"Please don't do that," said the artist, softly. "Of course I shouldn't have agreed with you. I beg pardon for having done so, but now that we are here, you are not to shirk your share of the duties. I want you to search around and get materials for a fire."

"Search around?" cried Miss Sommerton dolefully.

"Yes, search around. Hunt, as you Americans say. You have got us into this scrape, so I don't propose you shall sit calmly by and not take any of the consequences."

"Do you mean to insult me, Mr. Trenton, now that I am helpless?"

"If it is an insult to ask you to get up and gather some wood and bring it here, then I do mean to insult you most emphatically. I shall gather some, too, for we shall need a quantity of it."

Miss Sommerton rose indignantly, and was on the point of threatening to leave the place, when a moment's reflection showed her that she didn't know where to go, and remembering she was not as brave in the darkness and in the woods as in Boston, she meekly set about the search for dry twigs and sticks. Flinging down the bundle near the heap Trenton had already collected, the young woman burst into a laugh.

"Do you see anything particularly funny in the situation?" asked Trenton, with chattering teeth. "I confess I do not."

"The funniness of the situation is that we should gather wood, when, if there is a match in your pocket, it must be so wet as to be useless."

"Oh, not at all. You must remember I come from a very damp climate, and we take care of our matches there. I have been in the water before now on a tramp, and my matches are in a silver case warranted to keep out the wet." As he said this Trenton struck a light, and applied it to the small twigs and dry autumn leaves. The flames flashed up through the larger sticks, and in a very few moments a cheering fire was blazing, over which Trenton threw armful after armful of the wood he had collected.

"Now," said the artist, "if you will take off what outer wraps you have on, we can spread them here, and dry them. Then if you sit, first facing the fire and next with your back to it, and maintain a sort of rotatory motion, it will not be long before you are reasonably dry and warm."

Miss Sommerton laughed, but there was not much merriment in her laughter.

"Was there ever anything so supremely ridiculous?" she said. "A gentleman from England gathering sticks, and a lady from Boston gyrating before the fire. I am glad you are not a newspaper man, for you might be tempted to write about the situation for some sensational paper."

"How do you know I am not a journalist?"

"Well, I hope you are not. I thought you were a photographer."

"Oh, not a professional photographer, you know."

"I am sorry; I prefer the professional to the amateur."

"I like to hear you say that."

"Why? It is not very complimentary, I am sure."

"The very reason I like to hear you say it. If you were complimentary I would be afraid you were going to take a chill and be ill after this disaster; but now that you are yourself again, I have no such fear."

"Myself again!" blazed the young woman. "What do you know about me? How do you know whether I am myself or somebody else? I am sure our acquaintance has been very short."

"Counted by time, yes. But an incident like this, in the wilderness, does more to form a friendship, or the reverse, than years of ordinary acquaintance in Boston or London. You ask how I know that you are yourself. Shall I tell you?"

"If you please."

"Well, I imagine you are a young lady who has been spoilt. I think probably you are rich, and have had a good deal of your own way in this world. In fact, I take it for granted that you have never met any one who frankly told you your faults. Even if such good fortune had been yours, I doubt if you would have profited by it. A snub would have been the reward of the courageous person who told Miss Sommerton her failings."

"I presume you have courage enough to tell me my faults without the fear of a snub before your eyes."

"I have the courage, yes. You see I have already received the snub three or four times, and it has lost its terrors for me."

"In that case, will you be kind enough to tell me what you consider my faults?"

"If you wish me to."

"I do wish it."

"Well, then, one of them is inordinate pride."

"Do you think pride a fault?"

"It is not usually reckoned one of the virtues."

"In this country, Mr. Trenton, we consider that every person should have a certain amount of pride."

"A certain amount may be all right. It depends entirely on how much the certain amount is."

"Well, now for fault No. 2."

"Fault No. 2 is a disregard on your part for the feelings of others. This arises, I imagine, partly from fault No. 1. You are in the habit of classing the great mass of the public very much beneath you in intellect and other qualities, and you forget that persons whom you may perhaps dislike, have feelings which you have no right to ignore."

"I presume you refer to this morning," said Miss Sommerton, seriously. "I apologised for that two or three times, I think. I have always understood that a gentleman regards an apology from another gentleman as blotting out the original offence. Why should he not regard it in the same light when it comes from a woman?"

"Oh, now you are making a personal matter of it. I am talking in an entirely impersonal sense. I am merely giving you, with brutal rudeness, opinions formed on a very short acquaintance. Remember, I have done so at your own request."

"I am very much obliged to you, I am sure. I think you are more than half right. I hope the list is not much longer."

"No, the list ends there. I suppose you imagine that I am one of the rudest men you ever met?"

"No, we generally expect rudeness from Englishmen."

"Oh, do you really? Then I am only keeping up the reputation my countrymen have already acquired in America. Have you had the pleasure of meeting a rude Englishman before?"

"No, I can't say that I have. Most Englishmen I have met have been what we call very gentlemanly indeed. But the rudest letter I ever received was from an Englishman; not only rude, but ungrateful, for I had bought at a very high price one of his landscapes. He was John Trenton, the artist, of London. Do you know him?"

"Yes," hesitated Trenton, "I know him. I may say I know him very well. In fact, he is a namesake of mine."

"Why, how curious it is I had never thought of that. Is your first name J—, the same as his?"

"Yes."

"Not a relative, is he?"

"Well, no. I don't think I can call him a relative. I don't know that I can even go so far as to call him my friend, but he is an acquaintance."

"Oh, tell me about him," cried Miss Sommerton, enthusiastically. "He is one of the Englishmen I have longed very much to meet."

"Then you forgave him his rude letter?"

"Oh, I forgave that long ago. I don't know that it was rude, after all. It was truthful. I presume the truth offended me."

"Well," said Trenton, "truth has to be handled very delicately, or it is apt to give offence. You bought a landscape of his, did you? Which one, do you remember?"

"It was a picture of the Thames valley."

"Ah, I don't recall it at the moment. A rather hackneyed subject, too. Probably he sent it to America because he couldn't sell it in England."

"Oh, I suppose you think we buy anything here that the English refuse, I beg to inform you this picture had a place in the Royal Academy, and was very highly spoken of by the critics. I bought it in England."

"Oh yes, I remember it now, 'The Thames at Sonning.' Still, it was a hackneyed subject, although reasonably well treated."

"Reasonably well! I think it one of the finest landscape pictures of the century."

"Well, in that at least Trenton would agree with you."

"He is very conceited, you mean?"

"Even his enemies admit that."

"I don't believe it. I don't believe a man of such talent could be so conceited."

"Then, Miss Sommerton, allow me to say you have very little knowledge of human nature. It is only reasonable that a great man should know he is a great man. Most of our great men are conceited. I would like to see Trenton's letter to you. I could then have a good deal of amusement at his expense when I get back."

"Well, in that case I can assure you that you will never see the letter."

"Ah, you destroyed it, did you?"

"Not for that reason."

"Then you did destroy it?"

"I tore it up, but on second thoughts I pasted it together again, and have it still."

"In that case, why should you object to showing me the letter?"

"Well, because I think it rather unusual for a lady to be asked by a gentleman show him a letter that has been written to her by another gentleman."

"In matters of the heart that is true; but in matters of art it is not."

"Is that intended for a pun?"

"It is as near to one as I ever allow myself to come, I should like very much to see Mr. Trenton's letter. It was probably brutally rude. I know the man, you see."

"It was nothing of the sort," replied Miss Sommerton, hotly. "It was a truthful, well-meant letter."

"And yet you tore it up?"

"But that was the first impulse. The pasting it together was the apology."

"And you will not show it to me?"

"No, I will not."

"Did you answer it?"

"I will tell you nothing more about it. I am sorry I spoke of the letter at all. You don't appreciate Mr. Trenton's work."

"Oh, I beg your pardon, I do. He has no greater admirer in England than I am—except himself, of course."

"I suppose it makes no difference to you to know that I don't like a remark like that."

"Oh, I thought it would please you. You see, with the exception of myself, Mr. Trenton is about the rudest man in England. In fact, I begin to suspect it was Mr. Trenton's letter that led you to a wholesale condemning of the English race, for you admit the Englishmen you have met were not rude."

"You forget I have met you since then."

"Well bowled, as we say in cricket."

"Has Mr. Trenton many friends in London?"

"Not a great number. He is a man who sticks rather closely to his work, and, as I said before, he prides himself on telling the truth. That doesn't do in London any more than it does in Boston."

"Well, I honour him for it."

"Oh, certainly; everybody does in the abstract. But it is not a quality that tends to the making or the keeping of friends, you know."

"If you see Mr. Trenton when you return, I wish you would tell him there is a lady in America who is a friend of his; and if he has any pictures the people over there do not appreciate, ask him to send them to Boston, and his friend will buy them."

"Then you must be rich, for his pictures bring very good prices, even in England."

"Yes," said Miss Sommerton, "I am rich."

"Well, I suppose it's very jolly to be rich," replied the artist, with a sigh.

"You are not rich, then, I imagine?"

"No, I am not. That is, not compared with your American fortunes. I have enough of money to let me roam around the world if I wish to, and get half drowned in the St. Maurice River."

"Oh, is it not strange that we have heard nothing from those boatmen? You surely don't imagine they could have been drowned?"

"I hardly think so. Still, it is quite possible."

"Oh, don't say that; it makes me feel like a murderer."

"Well, I think it was a good deal your fault, don't you know." Miss Sommerton looked at him.

"Have I not been punished enough already?" she said.

"For the death of two men—if they are dead? Bless me! no. Do you imagine for a moment there is any relation between the punishment and the fault?"

Miss Sommerton buried her face in her hands.

"Oh, I take that back," said Trenton. "I didn't mean to say such a thing."

"It is the truth—it is the truth!" wailed the young woman. "Do you honestly think they did not reach the shore?"

"Of course they did. If you want to know what has happened, I'll tell you exactly, and back my opinion by a bet if you like. An Englishman is always ready to back his opinion, you know. Those two men swam with the current until they came to some landing-place. They evidently think we are drowned. Nevertheless, they are now making their way through the woods to the settlement. Then comes the hubbub. Mason will stir up the neighbourhood, and the men who are back from the woods with the other canoes will be roused and pressed into service, and some time to-night we will be rescued."

"Oh, I hope that is the case," cried Miss Sommerton, looking brightly at him.

"It is the case. Will you bet about it?"

"I never bet," said Miss Sommerton.

"Ah, well, you miss a good deal of fun then. You see I am a bit of a mind reader. I can tell just about where the men are now."

"I don't believe much in mind reading."

"Don't you? Shall I give you a specimen of it? Take that letter we have spoken so much about. If you think it over in your mind I will read you the letter—not word for word, perhaps, but I shall give you gist of it, at least."

"Oh, impossible!"

"Do you remember it?"

"I have it with me."

"Oh, have you? Then, if you wish to preserve it, you should spread it out upon the ground to dry before the fire."

"There is no need of my producing the letter," replied Miss Sommerton; "I remember every word it."

"Very well, just think it over in your mind, and see if I cannot repeat it. Are you thinking about it?"

"Yes, I am thinking about it."

"Here goes, then. 'Miss Edith Sommerton—'"

"Wrong," said that young lady.

"The Sommerton is right, is it not?"

"Yes, but the first name is not."

"What is it, then?"

"I shall not tell you."

"Oh, very well. Miss Sommerton,—'I have some hesitation in answering your letter.' Oh, by the way, I forgot the address. That is the first sentence of the letter, but the address is some number which I cannot quite see, 'Beacon Street, Boston.' Is there any such street in that city?"

"There is," said Miss Sommerton. "What a question to ask."

"Ah, then Beacon Street is one of the principal streets, is it?"

"One of them? It is the street. It is Boston."

"Very good. I will now proceed with the letter. 'I have some hesitation in answering your letter, because the sketches you send are so bad, that it seems to me no one could seriously forward them to an artist for criticism. However, if you really desire criticism, and if the pictures are sent in good faith, I may say I see in them no merit whatever, not even good drawing; while the colours are put on in a way that would seem to indicate you have not yet learned the fundamental principle of mixing the paints. If you are thinking of earning a livelihood with your pencil, I strongly advise you to abandon the idea. But if you are a lady of leisure and wealth, I suppose there is no harm in your continuing as long as you see fit.—Yours truly, JOHN TRENTON.'"

Miss Sommerton, whose eyes had opened wider and wider as this reading went on, said sharply—

"He has shown you the letter. You have seen it before it was sent."

"I admit that," said the artist.

58

"Well—I will believe all you like to say about Mr. John Trenton."

"Now, stop a moment; do not be too sweeping in your denunciation of him. I know that Mr. Trenton showed the letter to no one."

"Why, I thought you said a moment ago that he showed it to you."

"He did. Yet no one but himself saw the letter."

The young lady sprang to her feet.

"Are you, then, John Trenton, the artist?"

"Miss Sommerton, I have to plead guilty."

Chapter VI

Miss Eva Sommerton and Mr. John Trenton stood on opposite sides of the blazing fire and looked at each other. A faint smile hovered around the lips of the artist, but Miss Sommerton's face was very serious. She was the first to speak.

"It seems to me," she said, "that there is something about all this that smacks of false pretences."

"On my part, Miss Sommerton?"

"Certainly on your part. You must have known all along that I was the person who had written the letter to you. I think, when you found that out, you should have spoken of it."

"Then you do not give me credit for the honesty of speaking now. You ought to know that I need not have spoken at all, unless I wished to be very honest about the matter."

"Yes, there is that to be said in your favour, of course."

"Well, Miss Sommerton, I hope you will consider anything that happens to be in my favour. You see, we are really old friends, after all."

"Old enemies, you mean."

"Oh, I don't know about that. I would rather look on myself as your friend than your enemy."

"The letter you wrote me was not a very friendly one."

"I am not so sure. We differ on that point, you know."

"I am afraid we differ on almost every point."

"No, I differ with you there again. Still, I must admit I would prefer being your enemy—"

"To being my friend?" said Miss Sommerton, quickly.

"No, to being entirely indifferent to you."

"Really, Mr. Trenton, we are getting along very rapidly, are we not?" said the young lady, without looking up at him.

"Now, I am pleased to be able to agree with you there, Miss Sommerton. As I said before, an incident like this does more to ripen acquaintance or friendship, or—" The young man hesitated, and did not complete his sentence.

"Well," said the artist, after a pause, "which is it to be, friends or enemies?"

"It shall be exactly as you say," she replied.

"If you leave the choice to me, I shall say friends. Let us shake hands on that."

She held out her hand frankly to him as he crossed over to her side, and as he took it in his own, a strange thrill passed through him, and acting on the impulse of the moment, he drew her toward him and kissed her.

"How dare you!" she cried, drawing herself indignantly from him. "Do you think I am some backwoods girl who is flattered by your preference after a day's acquaintance?"

"Not a day's acquaintance, Miss Sommerton—a year, two years, ten years. In fact, I feel as though I had known you all my life."

"You certainly act as if you had. I did think for some time past that you were a gentleman. But you take advantage now of my unprotected position."

"Miss Sommerton, let me humbly apologise!"

"I shall not accept your apology. It cannot be apologised for. I must ask you not to speak to me again until Mr. Mason comes. You may consider yourself very fortunate when I tell you I shall say nothing of what has passed to Mr. Mason when he arrives."

John Trenton made no reply, but gathered another armful of wood and flung it on the fire.

Miss Sommerton sat very dejectedly looking at the embers.

For half an hour neither of them said anything.

Suddenly Trenton jumped up and listened intently.

"What is it?" cried Miss Sommerton, startled by his action.

"Now," said Trenton, "that is unfair. If I am not to be allowed to speak to you, you must not ask me any questions."

"I beg your pardon," said Miss Sommerton, curtly.

"But really I wanted to say something, and I wanted you to be the first to break the contract imposed. May I say what I wish to? I have just thought about something."

"If you have thought of anything that will help us out of our difficulty, I shall be very glad to hear it indeed."

"I don't know that it will help us out of our difficulties, but I think it will help us now that we're in them. You know, I presume, that my camera, like John Brown's knapsack, was strapped on my back, and that it is one of the few things rescued from the late disaster?"

He paused for a reply, but she said nothing. She evidently was not interested in his camera.

"Now, that camera-box is water-tight. It is really a very natty arrangement, although you regard it so scornfully."

He paused a second time, but there was no reply.

"Very well; packed in that box is, first the camera, then the dry plates, but most important of all, there are at least two or three very nice Three Rivers sandwiches. What do you say to our having supper?"

Miss Sommerton smiled in spite of herself, and Trenton busily unstrapped the camera-box, pulled out the little instrument, and fished up from the bottom a neatly-folded white table-napkin, in which were wrapped several sandwiches.

"Now," he continued, "I have a folding drinking-cup and a flask of sherry. It shows how absent-minded I am, for I ought to have thought of the wine long ago. You should have had a glass of sherry the moment we landed here. By the way, I wanted to say, and I say it now in case I shall forget it, that when I ordered you so unceremoniously to go around picking up sticks for the fire, it was not because I needed assistance, but to keep you, if possible, from getting a chill."

"Very kind of you," remarked Miss Sommerton.

But the Englishman could not tell whether she meant just what she said or not.

"I wish you would admit that you are hungry. Have you had anything to eat to-day?"

"I had, I am ashamed to confess," she answered. "I took lunch with me and I ate it coming down in the canoe. That was what troubled me about you. I was afraid you had eaten nothing all day, and I wished to offer you some lunch when we were in the canoe, but scarcely liked to. I thought we would soon reach the settlement. I am very glad you have sandwiches with you."

"How little you Americans really know of the great British nation, after all. Now, if there is one thing more than another that an Englishman looks after, it is the commissariat."

After a moment's silence he said—

"Don't you think, Miss Sommerton, that notwithstanding any accident or disaster, or misadventure that may have happened, we might get back at least on the old enemy footing again? I would like to apologise"—he paused for a moment, and added, "for the letter I wrote you ever so many years ago."

"There seem to be too many apologies between us," she replied. "I shall neither give nor take any more."

"Well," he answered, "I think after all that is the best way. You ought to treat me rather kindly though, because you are the cause of my being here."

"That is one of the many things I have apologised for. You surely do not wish to taunt me with it again?"

"Oh, I don't mean the recent accident. I mean being here in America. Your sketches of the Shawenegan Falls, and your description of the Quebec district, brought me out to America; and, added to that—I expected to meet you."

"To meet me?"

"Certainly. Perhaps you don't know that I called at Beacon Street, and found you were from home—with friends in Canada, they said—and I want to say, in self-defence, that I came very well introduced. I brought letters to people in Boston of the most undoubted respectability, and to people in New York, who are as near the social equals of the Boston people as it is possible for mere New York persons to be. Among other letters of introduction I had two to you. I saw the house in Beacon Street. So, you see, I have no delusions about your being a backwoods girl, as you charged me with having a short time since."

"I would rather not refer to that again, if you please."

"Very well. Now, I have one question to ask you—one request to make. Have I your permission to make it?"

"It depends entirely on what your request is."

"Of course, in that case you cannot tell until I make it. So I shall now make my request, and I want you to remember, before you refuse it, that you are indebted to me for supper. Miss Sommerton, give me a plug of tobacco."

Miss Sommerton stood up in dumb amazement.

"You see," continued the artist, paying no heed to her evident resentment, "I have lost my tobacco in the marine disaster, but luckily I have my pipe. I admit the scenery is beautiful here, if we could only see it; but darkness is all

64

around, although the moon is rising. It can therefore be no desecration for me to smoke a pipeful of tobacco, and I am sure the tobacco you keep will be the very best that can be bought. Won't you grant my request, Miss Sommerton?"

At first Miss Sommerton seemed to resent the audacity of this request. Then a conscious light came into her face, and instinctively her hand pressed the side of her dress where her pocket was supposed to be.

"Now," said the artist, "don't deny that you have the tobacco. I told you I was a bit of a mind reader, and besides, I have been informed that young ladies in America are rarely without the weed, and that they only keep the best."

The situation was too ridiculous for Miss Sommerton to remain very long indignant about it. So she put her hand in her pocket and drew out a plug of tobacco, and with a bow handed it to the artist.

"Thanks," he replied; "I shall borrow a pipeful and give you back the remainder. Have you ever tried the English birdseye? I assure you it is a very nice smoking tobacco."

"I presume," said Miss Sommerton, "the boatmen told you I always gave them some tobacco when I came up to see the falls?"

"Ah, you will doubt my mind-reading gift. Well, honestly, they did tell me, and I thought perhaps you might by good luck have it with you now. Besides, you know, wasn't there the least bit of humbug about your objection to smoking as we came up the river? If you really object to smoking, of course I shall not smoke now."

"Oh, I haven't the least objection to it. I am sorry I have not a good cigar to offer you."

"Thank you. But this is quite as acceptable. We rarely use plug tobacco in England, but I find some of it in this country is very good indeed."

"I must confess," said Miss Sommerton, "that I have very little interest in the subject of tobacco. But I cannot see why we should not have good tobacco in this country. We grow it here."

"That's so, when you come to think of it," answered the artist.

Trenton sat with his back against the tree, smoking in a meditative manner, and watching the flicker of the firelight on the face of his companion, whose thoughts seemed to be concentrated on the embers.

"Miss Sommerton," he said at last, "I would like permission to ask you a second question.

"You have it," replied that lady, without looking up. "But to prevent disappointment, I may say this is all the tobacco I have. The rest I left in the canoe when I went up to the falls."

"I shall try to bear the disappointment as well as I may. But in this case the question is of a very different nature. I don't know just exactly how to put it. You may have noticed that I am rather awkward when it comes to saying the right thing at the right time. I have not been much accustomed to society, and I am rather a blunt man."

"Many persons," said Miss Sommerton with some severity, "pride themselves on their bluntness. They seem to think it an excuse for saying rude things. There is a sort of superstition that bluntness and honesty go together."

"Well, that is not very encouraging, However, I do not pride myself on my bluntness, but rather regret it. I was merely stating a condition of things, not making a boast. In this instance I imagine I can show that honesty is the accompaniment. The question I wished to ask was something like this: Suppose I had had the chance to present to you my letters of introduction, and suppose that we had known each other for some time, and suppose that everything had been very conventional, instead of somewhat unconventional; supposing all this, would you have deemed a recent action of mine so unpardonable as you did a while ago?"

"You said you were not referring to smoking."

"Neither am I. I am referring to my having kissed you. There's bluntness for you."

"My dear sir," replied Miss Sommerton, shading her face with her hand, "you know nothing whatever of me."

"That is rather evading the question."

"Well, then, I know nothing whatever of you."

"That is the second evasion. I am taking it for granted that we each know something of the other."

"I should think it would depend entirely on how the knowledge influenced each party in the case. It is such a purely supposititious state of things that I cannot see how I can answer your question. I suppose you have heard the adage about not crossing a bridge until you come to it."

"I thought it was a stream."

"Well, a stream then. The principle is the same."'

"I was afraid I would not be able to put the question in a way to make you understand it. I shall now fall back on my bluntness again, and with this question, are you betrothed?"

"We generally call it engaged in this country."

"Then I shall translate my question into the language of the country, and ask if—"

"Oh, don't ask it, please. I shall answer before you do ask it by saying, No. I do not know why I should countenance your bluntness, as you call it, by giving you an answer to such a question; but I do so on condition that the question is the last."

"But the second question cannot be the last. There is always the third reading of a bill. The auctioneer usually cries, 'Third and last time,' not 'Second and last time,' and the banns of approaching marriage are called out three times. So, you see, I have the right to ask you one more question."

"Very well. A person may sometimes have the right to do a thing, and yet be very foolish in exercising that right."

"I accept your warning," said the artist, "and reserve my right."

"What time is it, do you think?" she asked him.

"I haven't the least idea," he replied; "my watch has stopped. That case was warranted to resist water, but I doubt if it has done so."

"Don't you think that if the men managed to save themselves they would have been here by this time?"

"I am sure I don't know. I have no idea of the distance. Perhaps they may have taken it for granted we are drowned, and so there is one chance in a thousand that they may not come back at all."

"Oh, I do not think such a thing is possible. The moment Mr. Mason heard of the disaster he would come without delay, no matter what he might believe the result of the accident to be."

"Yes, I think you are right. I shall try to get out on this point and see if I can discover anything of them. The moon now lights up the river, and if they are within a reasonable distance I think I can see them from this point of rock."

The artist climbed up on the point, which projected over the river. The footing was not of the safest, and Miss Sommerton watched him with some anxiety as he slipped and stumbled and kept his place by holding on to the branches of the overhanging trees.

"Pray be careful, Mr. Trenton," she said; "remember you are over the water there, and it is very swift."

"The rocks seem rather slippery with the dew," answered the artist; "but I am reasonably surefooted."

"Well, please don't take any chances; for, disagreeable as you are, I don't wish to be left here alone."

"Thank you, Miss Sommerton."

The artist stood on the point of rock, and, holding by a branch of a tree, peered out over the river.

"Oh, Mr. Trenton, don't do that!" cried the young lady, with alarm.

"Please come back."

"Say 'John,' then," replied the gentleman.

"Oh, Mr. Trenton, don't!" she cried as he leaned still further over the water, straining the branch to its utmost.

"Say 'John.'"

"Mr. Trenton."

"'John.'"

The branch cracked ominously as Trenton leaned yet a little further.

"John!" cried the young lady, sharply, "cease your fooling and come down from that rock."

The artist instantly recovered his position, and, coming back, sprang down to the ground again.

Miss Sommerton drew back in alarm; but Trenton merely put his hands in his pockets, and said—

"Well, Eva, I came back because you called me."

"It was a case of coercion," she said. "You English are too fond of coercion. We Americans are against it."

"Oh, I am a Home Ruler, if you are," replied the artist. "Miss Eva, I am going to risk my third and last question, and I shall await the answer with more anxiety than I ever felt before in my life. The question is this: Will—"

"Hello! there you are. Thank Heaven! I was never so glad to see anybody in my life," cried the cheery voice of Ed. Mason, as he broke through the bushes towards them.

Trenton looked around with anything but a welcome on his brow. If Mason had never been so glad in his life to see anybody, it was quite evident his feeling was not entirely reciprocated by the artist.

"How the deuce did you get here?" asked Trenton. "I was just looking for you down the river."

"Well, you see, we kept pretty close to the shore. I doubt if you could have seen us. Didn't you hear us shout?"

"No, we didn't hear anything. We didn't hear them shout, did we, Miss Sommerton?"

"No," replied that young woman, looking at the dying fire, whose glowing embers seemed to redden her face.

"Why, do you know," said Mason, "it looks as if you had been quarrelling. I guess I came just in the nick of time."

"You are always just in time, Mr. Mason," said Miss Sommerton. "For we were quarrelling, as you say. The subject of the quarrel is which of us was rightful owner of that canoe."

Mason laughed heartily, while Miss Sommerton frowned at him with marked disapprobation.

"Then you found me out, did you? Well, I expected you would before the day was over. You see, it isn't often that I have to deal with two such particular people in the same day. Still, I guess the ownership of the canoe doesn't amount to much now. I'll give it to the one who finds it."

"Oh, Mr. Mason," cried Miss Sommerton, "did the two men escape all right?"

"Why, certainly, I have just been giving them 'Hail Columbia,' because they didn't come back to you; but you see, a little distance down, the bank gets very steep—so much so that it is impossible to climb it, and then the woods here are thick and hard to work a person's way through. So they thought it best to come down and tell me, and we have brought two canoes up with us."

"Does Mrs. Mason know of the accident?"

"No, she doesn't; but she is just as anxious as if she did. She can't think what in the world keeps you."

"She doesn't realise," said the artist, "what strong attractions the

Shawenegan Falls have for people alive to the beauties of nature."

"Well," said Mason, "we mustn't stand here talking. You must be about frozen to death." Here he shouted to one of the men to come up and put out the fire.

"Oh, don't bother," said the artist; "it will soon burn out."

"Oh yes," put in Ed. Mason; "and if a wind should happen to rise in the night, where would my pine forest be? I don't propose to have a whole section of the country burnt up to commemorate the quarrel between you two."

The half-breed flung the biggest brand into the river, and speedily trampled out the rest, carrying up some water in his hat to pour on the centre of the fire. This done, they stepped into the canoe and were soon on their way down the river. Reaching the landing, the artist gave his hand to Miss Sommerton and aided her out on the bank.

"Miss Sommerton," he whispered to her, "I intended to sail to-morrow. I shall leave it for you to say whether I shall go or not."

"You will not sail," said Miss Sommerton promptly.

"Oh, thank you," cried the artist; "you do not know how happy that makes me."

"Why should it?"

"Well, you know what I infer from your answer."

"My dear sir, I said that you would not sail, and you will not, for this reason: To sail you require to catch to-night's train for Montreal, and take the train from there to New York to get your boat. You cannot catch to-night's train, and, therefore, cannot get to your steamer. I never before saw a man so glad to miss his train or his boat. Good-night, Mr. Trenton. Good-night, Mr. Mason," she cried aloud to that gentleman, as she disappeared toward the house.

"You two appear to be quite friendly," said Mr. Mason to the artist.

"Do we? Appearances are deceitful. I really cannot tell at this moment whether we are friends or enemies."

"Well, not enemies, I am sure. Miss Eva is a very nice girl when you understand her."

"Do you understand her?" asked the artist.

"I can't say that I do. Come to think of it, I don't think anybody does."

"In that case, then, for all practical purposes, she might just as well not be a nice girl."

"Ah, well, you may change your opinion some day—when you get better acquainted with her," said Mason, shaking hands with his friend. "And now that you have missed your train, anyhow, I don't suppose you care for a very early start to-morrow. Good-night."

Chapter VII

After Trenton awoke next morning he thought the situation over very calmly, and resolved to have question number three answered that day if possible.

When called to breakfast he found Ed. Mason at the head of the table.

"Shan't we wait for the ladies?" asked the artist.

"I don't think we'd better. You see we might have to wait quite a long time. I don't know when Miss Sommerton will be here again, and it will be a week at least before Mrs. Mason comes back. They are more than half-way to Three Rivers by this time."

"Good gracious!" cried Trenton, abashed; "why didn't you call me? I should have liked very much to have accompanied them."

"Oh, they wouldn't hear of your being disturbed; and besides, Mr. Trenton, our American ladies are quite in the habit of looking after themselves. I found that out long ago."

"I suppose there is nothing for it but get out my buckboard and get back to Three Rivers."

"Oh, I dismissed your driver long ago," said the lumberman. "I'll take you there in my buggy. I am going out to Three Rivers to-day anyhow."

"No chance of overtaking the ladies?" asked Trenton.

"I don't think so. We may overtake Mrs. Mason but I imagine Miss Sommerton will be either at Quebec or Montreal before we reach Three Rivers. I don't know in which direction she is going. You seem to be somewhat interested in that young lady. Purely artistic admiration, I presume. She is rather a striking girl. Well, you certainly have made the most of your opportunities. Let's see, you have known her now for quite a long while. Must be nearly twenty-four hours."

"Oh, don't underestimate it, Mason; quite thirty-six hours at least."

"So long as that? Ah, well, I don't wish to discourage you; but I wouldn't be too sure of her if I were you."

"Sure of her! Why, I am not sure of anything."

"Well, that is the proper spirit. You Englishmen are rather apt to take things for granted. I think you would make a mistake in this case if you were too sure. You are not the only man who has tried to awaken the interest of Miss Sommerton of Boston."

"I didn't suppose that I was. Nevertheless, I am going to Boston."

"Well, it's a nice town," said Mason, with a noncommittal air. "It hasn't the advantages of Three Rivers, of course; but still it is a very attractive place in some respects."

"In some respects, yes," said the artist.

* * * * *

Two days later Mr. John Trenton called at the house on Beacon Street.

"Miss Sommerton is not at home," said the servant. "She is in Canada somewhere."

And so Mr. Trenton went back to his hotel.

The artist resolved to live quietly in Boston until Miss Sommerton returned. Then the fateful number three could be answered. He determined not to present any of his letters of introduction. When he came to Boston first, he thought he would like to see something of society, of the art world in that city, if there was an art world, and of the people; but he had come and gone without being invited anywhere, and now he anticipated no trouble in living a quiet life, and thinking occasionally over the situation. But during his absence it appeared Boston had awakened to the fact that in its midst had resided a real live artist of prominence from the other side, and nothing had been done to overcome his prejudices, and show him that, after all, the real intellectual centre of the world was not London, but the capital of

Massachusetts.

The first day he spent in his hotel he was called upon by a young gentleman whose card proclaimed him a reporter on one of the large daily papers.

"You are Mr. Trenton, the celebrated English artist, are you not?"

"My name is Trenton, and by profession I am an artist. But I do not claim the adjective, 'celebrated.'"

"All right. You are the man I am after. Now, I should like to know what you think of the art movement in America?"

"Well, really, I have been in America but a very short time, and during that time I have had no opportunity of seeing the work of your artists or of visiting any collections, so you see I cannot give an opinion."

"Met any of our American artists?"

"I have in Europe, yes. Quite a number of them, and very talented gentlemen some of them are, too."

"I suppose Europe lays over this country in the matter of art, don't it?"

"I beg your pardon."

"Knocks the spots out of us in pictures?"

"I don't know that I quite follow you. Do you mean that we produce pictures more rapidly than you do here?"

"No, I just mean the whole tout ensemble of the thing. They are 'way ahead of us, are they not, in art?"

"Well, you see, as I said before—really, I am not in a position to make any comparison, because I am entirely ignorant of American painting. It seems to me that certain branches of art ought to flourish here. There is no country in the world with grander scenery than America."

"Been out to the Rockies?"

"Where is that?"

"To the Rocky Mountains?"

"Oh no, no. You see I have been only a few weeks in this country. I have confined my attention to Canada mainly, the Quebec region and around there, although I have been among the White Mountains, and the Catskills, and the Adirondacks."

"What school of art do you belong to?"

"School? Well, I don't know that I belong to any. May I ask if you are a connoisseur in art matters. Are you the art critic of your journal?"

"Me? No—oh no. I don't know the first darn thing about it. That's why they sent me."

"Well, I should have thought, if he wished to get anything worth publishing, your editor would have sent somebody who was at least familiar with the subject he has to write about."

"I dare say; but, that ain't the way to get snappy articles written. You take an art man, now, for instance; he's prejudiced. He thinks one school is all right, and another school isn't; and he is apt to work in his own fads. Now, if our man liked the French school, and despised the English school, or the German school, if there is one, or the Italian school, whatever it happened to be, and you went against that; why, don't you see, he would think you didn't know anything, and write you up that way. Now, I am perfectly unprejudiced. I want to write a good readable article, and I don't care a hang which school is the best or the worst, or anything else about it."

"Ah! I see. Well, in that case, you certainly approach your work without bias."

"You bet I do. Now, who do you think is the best painter in England?"

"In what line?"

"Well, in any line. Who stands ahead? Who's the leader? Who tops them all? Who's the Raphael?"

76

"I don't know that we have any Raphael? We have good painters each in his own branch."

"Isn't there one, in your opinion, that is 'way ahead of all the rest?"

"Well, you see, to make an intelligent comparison, you have to take into consideration the specialty of the painter. You could hardly compare Alma Tadema, for instance, with Sir John Millais, or Sir Frederic Leighton with Hubert Herkomer, or any of them with some of your own painters. Each has his specialty, and each stands at the head of it."

"Then there is no one man in England like Old Man Rubens, or Van Dyke, or those other fellows, I forget their names, who are head and shoulders above everybody else? Sort of Jay Gould in art, you know."

"No, I wouldn't like to say there is. In fact, all of your questions require some consideration. Now, if you will write them down for me, and give me time to think them over, I will write out such answers as occur to me. It would be impossible for me to do justice to myself, or to art, or to your paper, by attempting to answer questions off-hand in this way."

"Oh, that's too slow for our time here. You know this thing comes out to-morrow morning, and I have got to do a column and a half of it. Sometimes, you know, it is very difficult; but you are different from most Englishmen I have talked with. You speak right out, and you talk to a fellow. I can make a column and a half out of what you have said now."

"Dear me! Can you really? Well, now, I should be careful, if I were you. I am afraid that, if you don't understand anything about art, you may give the public some very erroneous impressions."

"Oh, the public don't care a hang. All they want is to read something snappy and bright. That's what the public want. No, sir, we have catered too long for the public not to know what its size is. You might print the most learned article you could get hold of, it might be written by What's-his-name De Vinci, and be full of art slang, and all that sort of thing, but it wouldn't touch the general public at all."

"I don't suppose it would."

"What do you think of our Sunday papers here? You don't have any Sunday papers over in London."

"Oh yes, we do. But none of the big dailies have Sunday editions."

"They are not as big, or as enterprising as ours, are they? One Sunday paper, you know, prints about as much as two or three thirty-five cent magazines."

"What, the Sunday paper does?"

"Yes, the Sunday paper prints it, but doesn't sell for that. We give 'em more for the money than any magazine you ever saw."

"You certainly print some very large papers."

With this the reporter took his leave, and next morning Mr. Trenton saw the most astonishing account of his ideas on art matters imaginable. What struck him most forcibly was, that an article written by a person who admittedly knew nothing at all about art should be in general so free from error. The interview had a great number of head lines, and it was evident the paper desired to treat the artist with the utmost respect, and that it felt he showed his sense in preferring Boston to New York as a place of temporary residence; but what appalled him was the free and easy criticisms he was credited with having made on his own contemporaries in England. The principal points of each were summed up with a great deal of terseness and force, and in many cases were laughably true to life. It was evident that whoever touched up that interview possessed a very clear opinion and very accurate knowledge of the art movement in England.

Mr. Trenton thought he would sit down and write to the editor of the paper, correcting some of the more glaring inaccuracies; but a friend said—

"Oh, it is no use. Never mind. Nobody pays any attention to that. It's all right anyhow."

"Yes, but suppose the article should be copied in England, or suppose some of the papers should get over there?"

"Oh, that'll be all right," said his friend, with easy optimism. "Don't bother about it. They all know what a newspaper interview is; if they don't, why, you can tell them when you get back."

It was not long before Mr. Trenton found himself put down at all the principal clubs, both artistic and literary; and he also became, with a suddenness that bewildered him, quite the social lion for the time being. He was astonished to find that the receptions to which he was invited, and where he was, in a way, on exhibition, were really very grand occasions, and compared favourably with the finest gatherings he had had experience of in London.

His hostess at one of these receptions said to him, "Mr. Trenton, I want to introduce you to some of our art lovers in this city, whom I am sure you will be pleased to meet. I know that as a general thing the real artists are apt to despise the amateurs; but in this instance I hope you will be kind enough not to despise them, for my sake. We think they are really very clever indeed, and we like to be flattered by foreign preference."

"Am I the foreign preference in this instance?"

"You are, Mr. Trenton."

"Now, I think it is too bad of you to say that, just when I have begun to feel as much at home in Boston as I do in London. I assure you I do not feel in the least foreign here. Neither do I maintain, like Mrs. Brown, that you are the foreigners."

"How very nice of you to say so, Mr. Trenton. Now I hope you will say something like that to the young lady I want you to meet. She is really very charming, and I am sure you will like her; and I may say, in parenthesis, that she, like the rest of us, is perfectly infatuated with your pictures."

As the lady said this, she brought Mr. Trenton in her wake, as it were, and said, "Miss Sommerton, allow me to present to you Mr. Trenton."

Miss Sommerton rose with graceful indolence, and held out her hand frankly to the artist. "Mr. Trenton," she said, "I am very pleased indeed to meet you. Have you been long in Boston?"

"Only a few days," replied Trenton. "I came up to Boston from Canada a short time since."

"Up? You mean down. We don't say up from Canada."

"Oh, don't you? Well, in England, you know, we say up to London, no matter from what part of the country we approach it. I think you are wrong in saying down, I think it really ought to be up to Boston from wherever you come."

His hostess appeared to be delighted with this bit of conversation, and she said, "I shall leave you two together for a few moments to get acquainted. Mr. Trenton, you know you are in demand this evening."

"Do you think that is true?" said Trenton to Miss Sommerton.

"What?"

"Well, that I am in demand."

"I suppose it is true, if Mrs. Lennox says it is. You surely don't intend to cast any doubt on the word of your hostess, do you?"

"Oh, not at all. I didn't mean in a general way, you know, I meant in particular."

"I don't think I understand you, Mr. Trenton. By the way, you said you had been in Canada. Do you not think it is a very charming country?"

"Charming, Miss Sommerton, isn't the word for it. It is the most delightful country in the world."

"Ah, you say that because it belongs to England. I admit it is very delightful; but then there are other places on the Continent quite as beautiful as any part of Canada. You seem to have a prejudice in favour of monarchical institutions."

"Oh, is Canada monarchical? I didn't know that. I thought Canada was quite republican in its form of government."

"Well, it is a dependency; that's what I despise about Canada. Think of a glorious country like that, with hundreds of thousands of square miles, in fact, millions, I think, being dependent on a little island, away there among the fogs and rains, between the North Sea and the Atlantic Ocean. To be a dependency of some splendid tyrannical power like Russia wouldn't be so bad; but to be dependent on that little island—I lose all my respect for Canada when I think of it."

"Well, you know, the United States were colonies once."

"Ah, that is a very unfortunate comparison, Mr. Trenton. The moment the colonies, as you call them, came to years of discretion, they soon shook off their dependency. You must remember you are at Boston, and that the harbour is only a short distance from here."

"Does that mean that I should take advantage of its proximity and leave?"

"Oh, not at all. I could not say anything so rude, Mr. Trenton. Perhaps you are not familiar with the history of our trouble with England? Don't you remember it commenced in Boston Harbour practically?"

"Oh yes, I recollect now. I had forgotten it. Something about tea, was it not?"

"Yes, something about tea."

"Well, talking of tea, Miss Sommerton, may I take you to the conservatory and bring you a cup of it?"

"May I have an ice instead of the tea, if I prefer it, Mr. Trenton?"

"Why, certainly. You see how I am already dropping into the American phraseology."

"Oh, I think you are improving wonderfully, Mr. Trenton."

When they reached the conservatory, Miss Sommerton said—

"This is really a very great breach of good manners on both your part and mine. I have taken away the lion of the evening, and the lion has forgotten his duty to his hostess and to the other guests."

"Well, you see, I wanted to learn more of your ideas in the matter of dependencies. I don't at all agree with you on that. Now, I think if a country is conquered, it ought to be a dependency of the conquering people. It is the right of conquest. I—I am a thorough believer in the right of conquest."

"You seem to have very settled opinions on the matter, Mr. Trenton."

"I have indeed, Miss Sommerton. It is said that an Englishman never knows when he is conquered. Now I think that is a great mistake. There is no one so quick as an Englishman to admit that he has met his match."

"Why, have you met your match already, Mr. Trenton? Let me congratulate you."

"Well, don't congratulate me just yet. I am not at all certain whether I shall need any congratulations or not."

"I am sure I hope you will be very successful."

"Do you mean that?"

Miss Sommerton looked at him quietly for a moment.

"Do you think," she said, "I am in the habit of saying things I do not mean?"

"I think you are."

"Well, you are not a bit more complimentary than—than—you used to be."

"You were going to say than I was on the banks of the St. Maurice?"

"Oh, you visited the St. Maurice, did you? How far away from Boston that seems, doesn't it?"

"It is indeed a great distance, Miss Sommerton. But apparently not half as long as the round-about way we are traveling just now. Miss Sommerton, I waited and waited in Boston for you to return. I want to be a dependence. I admit the conquest. I wish to swear fealty to Miss Eva Sommerton of Boston, and now I ask my third question, will you accept the allegiance?"

Miss Sommerton was a little slow in replying, and before she had spoken Mrs. Lennox bustled in, and said—

"Oh, Mr. Trenton, I have been looking everywhere for you. There are a hundred people here who wish to be introduced, and all at once. May I have him, Miss Sommerton?"

"Well, Mrs. Lennox, you know, if I said 'Yes,' that would imply a certain ownership in him."

"I brought Miss Sommerton here to get her to accept an ice from me, which as yet I have not had the privilege of bringing. Will you accept—the ice, Miss Sommerton?"

The young lady blushed, as she looked at the artist.

"Yes," she said with a sigh; the tone was almost inaudible.

The artist hurried away to bring the refreshment.

"Why, Eva Sommerton," cried Mrs. Lennox, "you accept a plate of ice cream as tragically as if you were giving the answer to a proposal."

Mrs. Lennox said afterward that she thought there was something very peculiar about Miss Sommerton's smile in reply to her remark.

FROM WHOSE BOURNE

CHAPTER I.

"My dear," said William Brenton to his wife, "do you think I shall be missed if I go upstairs for a while? I am not feeling at all well."

"Oh, I'm so sorry, Will," replied Alice, looking concerned; "I will tell them you are indisposed."

"No, don't do that," was the answer; "they are having a very good time, and I suppose the dancing will begin shortly; so I don't think they will miss me. If I feel better I will be down in an hour or two; if not, I shall go to bed. Now, dear, don't worry; but have a good time with the rest of them."

William Brenton went quietly upstairs to his room, and sat down in the darkness in a rocking chair. Remaining there a few minutes, and not feeling any better, he slowly undressed and went to bed. Faint echoes reached him of laughter and song; finally, music began, and he felt, rather than heard, the pulsation of dancing feet. Once, when the music had ceased for a time, Alice tiptoed into the room, and said in a quiet voice—

"How are you feeling, Will? any better?"

"A little," he answered drowsily. "Don't worry about me; I shall drop off to sleep presently, and shall be all right in the morning. Good night."

He still heard in a dreamy sort of way the music, the dancing, the laughter; and gradually there came oblivion, which finally merged into a dream, the most strange and vivid vision he had ever experienced. It seemed to him that he sat again in the rocking chair near the bed. Although he knew the room was dark, he had no difficulty in seeing everything perfectly. He heard, now quite plainly, the music and dancing downstairs, but what gave a ghastly significance to his dream was the sight of his own person on the bed. The eyes were half open, and the face was drawn and rigid. The colour of the face was the white, greyish tint of death.

"This is a nightmare," said Brenton to himself; "I must try and wake myself." But he seemed powerless to do this, and he sat there looking at his own body while the night wore on. Once he rose and went to the side of the bed. He seemed to have reached it merely by wishing himself there, and he passed his hand over the face, but no feeling of touch was communicated to him. He hoped his wife would come and rouse him from this fearful semblance of a dream, and, wishing this, he found himself standing at her side, amidst the throng downstairs, who were now merrily saying good-bye. Brenton tried to speak to his wife, but although he was conscious of speaking, she did not seem to hear him, or know he was there.

The party had been one given on Christmas Eve, and as it was now two o'clock in the morning, the departing guests were wishing Mrs. Brenton a merry Christmas. Finally, the door closed on the last of the revellers, and Mrs. Brenton stood for a moment giving instructions to the sleepy servants; then, with a tired sigh, she turned and went upstairs, Brenton walking by her side until they came to the darkened room, which she entered on tiptoe.

"Now," said Brenton to himself, "she will arouse me from this appalling dream." It was not that there was anything dreadful in the dream itself, but the clearness with which he saw everything, and the fact that his mind was perfectly wide awake, gave him an uneasiness which he found impossible to shake off.

In the dim light from the hall his wife prepared to retire. The horrible thought struck Brenton that she imagined he was sleeping soundly, and was anxious not to awaken him—for of course she could have no realization of the nightmare he was in—so once again he tried to communicate with her. He spoke her name over and over again, but she proceeded quietly with her preparations for the night. At last she crept in at the other side of the bed, and in a few moments was asleep. Once more Brenton struggled to awake, but with no effect. He heard the clock strike three, and then four, and then five, but there was no apparent change in his dream. He feared that he might be in a trance, from which, perhaps, he would not awake until it was too late. Grey daylight began to brighten the window, and he noticed that snow was quietly falling outside, the flakes noiselessly beating against the window pane. Every one slept late that morning, but at last he heard the preparations for breakfast going on downstairs—the light clatter of china on the table, the rattle of the grate; and, as he thought of these things, he found himself in the dining-room, and saw the trim little maid, who still yawned every now and then, laying the plates in their places. He went upstairs again, and stood watching the sleeping face of his wife. Once she raised her hand above her head, and he thought she was going to awake; ultimately her eyes opened, and she gazed for a time at the ceiling, seemingly trying to recollect the events of the day before.

"Will," she said dreamily, "are you still asleep?"

There was no answer from the rigid figure at the front of the bed. After a few moments she placed her hand quietly over the sleeper's face. As she did so, her startled eyes showed that she had received a shock. Instantly she sat upright in bed, and looked for one brief second on the face of the sleeper beside her; then, with a shriek that pierced the stillness of the room, she sprang to the floor.

"Will! Will!" she cried, "speak to me! What is the matter with you? Oh, my God! my God!" she cried, staggering back from the bed. Then, with shriek after shriek, she ran blindly through the hall to the stairway, and there fell fainting on the floor.

CHAPTER II.

William Brenton knelt beside the fallen lady, and tried to soothe and comfort her, but it was evident that she was insensible.

"It is useless," said a voice by his side.

Brenton looked up suddenly, and saw standing beside him a stranger. Wondering for a moment how he got there, and thinking that after all it was a dream, he said—

"What is useless? She is not dead."

"No," answered the stranger, "but you are."

"I am what?" cried Brenton.

"You are what the material world calls dead, although in reality you have just begun to live."

"And who are you?" asked Brenton. "And how did you get in here?"

The other smiled.

"How did you get in here?" he said, repeating Brenton's words.

"I? Why, this is my own house."

"Was, you mean."

"I mean that it is. I am in my own house. This lady is my wife."

"Was," said the other.

"I do not understand you," cried Brenton, very much annoyed. "But, in any case, your presence and your remarks are out of place here."

"My dear sir," said the other, "I merely wish to aid you and to explain to you anything that you may desire to know about your new condition. You are now free from the incumbrance of your body. You have already had some experience of the additional powers which that riddance has given you. You have also, I am afraid, had an inkling of the fact that the spiritual condition has its limitations. If you desire to communicate with those whom you have left, I would strongly advise you to postpone the attempt, and to leave this place, where you will experience only pain and anxiety. Come with me, and learn something of your changed circumstances."

"I am in a dream," said Brenton, "and you are part of it. I went to sleep last night, and am still dreaming. This is a nightmare and it will soon be over."

"You are saying that," said the other, "merely to convince yourself. It is now becoming apparent to you that this is not a dream. If dreams exist, it was a dream which you left, but you have now become awake. If you really think it is a dream, then do as I tell you—come with me and leave it, because you must admit that this part of the dream is at least very unpleasant."

"It is not very pleasant," assented Brenton. As he spoke the bewildered servants came rushing up the stairs, picked up their fallen mistress, and laid her on a sofa. They rubbed her hands and dashed water in her face. She opened her eyes, and then closed them again with a shudder.

"Sarah," she cried, "have I been dreaming, or is your master dead?"

The two girls turned pale at this, and the elder of them went boldly into the room which her mistress had just left. She was evidently a young woman who had herself under good control, but she came out sobbing, with her apron to her eyes.

"Come, come," said the man who stood beside Brenton, "haven't you had enough of this? Come with me; you can return to this house if you wish;" and together they passed out of the room into the crisp air of Christmas morning. But, although Brenton knew it must be cold, he had no feeling of either cold or warmth.

"There are a number of us," said the stranger to Brenton, "who take turns at watching the sick-bed when a man is about to die, and when his spirit leaves his body, we are there to explain, or comfort, or console. Your death was so sudden that we had no warning of it. You did not feel ill before last night, did you?"

"No," replied Brenton. "I felt perfectly well, until after dinner last night."

"Did you leave your affairs in reasonably good order?"

"Yes," said Brenton, trying to recollect. "I think they will find everything perfectly straight."

"Tell me a little of your history, if you do not mind," inquired the other; "it will help me in trying to initiate you into our new order of things here."

"Well," replied Brenton, and he wondered at himself for falling so easily into the other's assumption that he was a dead man, "I was what they call on the earth in reasonably good circumstances. My estate should be worth $100,000. I had $75,000 insurance on my life, and if all that is paid, it should net my widow not far from a couple of hundred thousand."

"How long have you been married?" said the other.

"Only about six months. I was married last July, and we went for a trip abroad. We were married quietly, and left almost immediately afterwards, so we thought, on our return, it would not be a bad plan to give a Christmas Eve dinner, and invite some of our friends. That," he said, hesitating a moment, "was last night. Shortly after dinner, I began to feel rather ill, and went upstairs to rest for a while; and if what you say is true, the first thing I knew I found myself dead."

"Alive," corrected the other.

"Well, alive, though at present I feel I belong more to the world I have left than I do to the world I appear to be in. I must confess, although you are a very plausible gentleman to talk to, that I expect at any moment to wake and find this to have been one of the most horrible nightmares that I ever had the ill luck to encounter."

The other smiled.

"There is very little danger of your waking up, as you call it. Now, I will tell you the great trouble we have with people when they first come to the spirit-land, and that is to induce them to forget entirely the world they have relinquished. Men whose families are in poor circumstances, or men whose affairs are in a disordered state, find it very difficult to keep from trying to set things right again. They have the feeling that they can console or comfort those whom they have left behind them, and it is often a long time before they are convinced that their efforts are entirely futile, as well as very distressing for themselves."

"Is there, then," asked Brenton, "no communication between this world and the one that I have given up?"

The other paused for a moment before he replied.

"I should hardly like to say," he answered, "that there is no communication between one world and the other; but the communication that exists is so slight and unsatisfactory, that if you are sensible you will see things with the eyes of those who have very much more experience in this world than you have. Of course, you can go back there as much as you like; there will be no interference and no hindrance. But when you see things going wrong, when you see a mistake about to be made, it is an appalling thing to stand there helpless, unable to influence those you love, or to point out a palpable error, and convince them that your clearer sight sees it as such. Of course, I understand that it must be very difficult for a man who is newly married, to entirely abandon the one who has loved him, and whom he loves. But I assure you that if you follow the life of one who is as young and handsome as your wife, you will find some one else supplying the consolations you are unable to bestow. Such a mission may lead you to a church where she is married to her second husband. I regret to say that even the most imperturbable spirits are ruffled when such an incident occurs. The wise men are those who appreciate and understand that they are in an entirely new world, with new powers and new limitations, and who govern themselves accordingly from the first, as they will certainly do later on."

"My dear sir," said Brenton, somewhat offended, "if what you say is true, and I am really a dead man——"

"Alive," corrected the other.

"Well, alive, then. I may tell you that my wife's heart is broken. She will never marry again."

"Of course, that is a subject of which you know a great deal more than I do. I all the more strongly advise you never to see her again. It is impossible for you to offer any consolation, and the sight of her grief and misery will only result in unhappiness for yourself. Therefore, take my advice. I have given it very often, and I assure you those who did not take it expressed their regret afterwards. Hold entirely aloof from anything relating to your former life."

Brenton was silent for some moments; finally he said—

"I presume your advice is well meant; but if things are as you state, then I may as well say, first as last, that I do not intend to accept it."

"Very well," said the other; "it is an experience that many prefer to go through for themselves."

"Do you have names in this spirit-land?" asked Brenton, seemingly desirous of changing the subject.

"Yes," was the answer; "we are known by names that we have used in the preparatory school below. My name is Ferris."

"And if I wish to find you here, how do I set about it?"

"The wish is sufficient," answered Ferris. "Merely wish to be with me, and you are with me."

"Good gracious!" cried Brenton, "is locomotion so easy as that?"

"Locomotion is very easy. I do not think anything could be easier than it is, and I do not think there could be any improvement in that matter."

"Are there matters here, then, that you think could be improved?"

"As to that I shall not say. Perhaps you will be able to give your own opinion before you have lived here much longer."

"Taking it all in all," said Brenton, "do you think the spirit-land is to be preferred to the one we have left?"

"I like it better," said Ferris, "although I presume there are some who do not. There are many advantages; and then, again, there are many—well, I would not say disadvantages, but still some people consider them such. We are free from the pangs of hunger or cold, and have therefore no need of money, and there is no necessity for the rush and the worry of the world below."

"And how about heaven and hell?" said Brenton. "Are those localities all a myth? Is there nothing of punishment and nothing of reward in this spirit-land?"

There was no answer to this, and when Brenton looked around he found that his companion had departed.

CHAPTER III.

William Brenton pondered long on the situation. He would have known better how to act if he could have been perfectly certain that he was not still the victim of a dream. However, of one thing there was no doubt—namely, that it was particularly harrowing to see what he had seen in his own house. If it were true that he was dead, he said to himself, was not the plan outlined for him by Ferris very much the wiser course to adopt? He stood now in one of the streets of the city so familiar to him. People passed and repassed him—men and women whom he had known in life—but nobody appeared to see him. He resolved, if possible, to solve the problem uppermost in his mind, and learn whether or not he could communicate with an inhabitant of the world he had left. He paused for a moment to consider the best method of doing this. Then he remembered one of his most confidential friends and advisers, and at once wished himself at his office. He found the office closed, but went in to wait for his friend. Occupying the time in thinking over his strange situation, he waited long, and only when the bells began to ring did he remember it was Christmas forenoon, and that his friend would not be at the office that day. The next moment he wished himself at his friend's house, but he was as unsuccessful as at the office; the friend was not at home. The household, however, was in great commotion, and, listening to what was said, he found that the subject of conversation was his own death, and he learned that his friend had gone to the Brenton residence as soon as he heard the startling news of Christmas morning.

Once more Brenton paused, and did not know what to do. He went again into the street. Everything seemed to lead him toward his own home. Although he had told Ferris that he did not intend to take his advice, yet as a sensible man he saw that the admonition was well worth considering, and if he could once become convinced that there was no communication possible between himself and those he had left; if he could give them no comfort and no cheer; if he could see the things which they did not see, and yet be unable to give them warning, he realized that he would merely be adding to his own misery, without alleviating the troubles of others.

He wished he knew where to find Ferris, so that he might have another talk with him. The man impressed him as being exceedingly sensible. No sooner, however, had he wished for the company of Mr. Ferris than he found himself beside that gentleman.

"By George!" he said in astonishment, "you are just the man I wanted to see."

"Exactly," said Ferris; "that is the reason you do see me."

"I have been thinking over what you said," continued the other, "and it strikes me that after all your advice is sensible."

"Thank you," replied Ferris, with something like a smile on his face.

"But there is one thing I want to be perfectly certain about. I want to know whether it is not possible for me to communicate with my friends. Nothing will settle that doubt in my mind except actual experience."

"And have you not had experience enough?" asked Ferris.

"Well," replied the other, hesitating, "I have had some experience, but it seems to me that, if I encounter an old friend, I could somehow make myself felt by him."

"In that case," answered Ferris, "if nothing will convince you but an actual experiment, why don't you go to some of your old friends and try what you can do with them?"

"I have just been to the office and to the residence of one of my old friends. I found at his residence that he had gone to my"—Brenton paused for a moment—"former home. Everything seems to lead me there, and yet, if I take your advice, I must avoid that place of all others."

"I would at present, if I were you," said Ferris. "Still, why not try it with any of the passers-by?"

Brenton looked around him. People were passing and repassing where the two stood talking with each other. "Merry Christmas" was the word on all lips. Finally Brenton said, with a look of uncertainty on his face—

"My dear fellow, I can't talk to any of these people. I don't know them."

Ferris laughed at this, and replied—

"I don't think you will shock them very much; just try it."

"Ah, here's a friend of mine. You wait a moment, and I will accost him." Approaching him, Brenton held out his hand and spoke, but the traveller paid no attention. He passed by as one who had seen or heard nothing.

"I assure you," said Ferris, as he noticed the look of disappointment on the other's face, "you will meet with a similar experience, however much you try. You know the old saying about one not being able to have his cake and eat it too. You can't have the privileges of this world and those of the world you left as well. I think, taking it all in all, you should rest content, although it always hurts those who have left the other world not to be able to communicate with their friends, and at least assure them of their present welfare."

"It does seem to me," replied Brenton, "that would be a great consolation, both for those who are here and those who are left."

"Well, I don't know about that," answered the other. "After all, what does life in the other world amount to? It is merely a preparation for this. It is of so short a space, as compared with the life we live here, that it is hardly worth while to interfere with it one way or another. By the time you are as long here as I have been, you will realize the truth of this."

"Perhaps I shall," said Brenton, with a sigh; "but, meanwhile, what am I to do with myself? I feel like the man who has been all his life in active business, and who suddenly resolves to enjoy himself doing nothing. That sort of thing seems to kill a great number of men, especially if they put off taking a rest until too late, as most of us do."

"Well," said Ferris, "there is no necessity of your being idle here, I assure you. But before you lay out any work for yourself, let me ask you if there is not some interesting part of the world that you would like to visit?"

"Certainly; I have seen very little of the world. That is one of my regrets at leaving it."

"Bless me," said the other, "you haven't left it."

"Why, I thought you said I was a dead man?"

"On the contrary," replied his companion, "I have several times insisted that you have just begun to live. Now where shall we spend the day?"

"How would London do?"

"I don't think it would do; London is apt to be a little gloomy at this time of the year. But what do you say to Naples, or Japan, or, if you don't wish to go out of the United States, Yellowstone Park?"

"Can we reach any of those places before the day is over?" asked Brenton, dubiously.

"Well, I will soon show you how we manage all that. Just wish to accompany me, and I will take you the rest of the way."

"How would Venice do?" said Brenton. "I didn't see half as much of that city as I wanted to."

"Very well," replied his companion, "Venice it is;" and the American city in which they stood faded away from them, and before Brenton could make up his mind exactly what was happening, he found himself walking with his comrade in St. Mark's Square.

"Well, for rapid transit," said Brenton, "this beats anything I've ever had any idea of; but it increases the feeling that I am in a dream."

"You'll soon get used to it," answered Ferris; "and, when you do, the cumbersome methods of travel in the world itself will show themselves in their right light. Hello!" he cried, "here's a man whom I should like you to meet. By the way, I either don't know your name or I have forgotten it."

"William Brenton," answered the other.

"Mr. Speed, I want to introduce you to Mr. Brenton."

"Ah," said Speed, cordially, "a new-comer. One of your victims, Ferris?"

"Say one of his pupils, rather," answered Brenton.

"Well, it is pretty much the same thing," said Speed. "How long have you been with us, and how do you like the country?"

"You see, Mr. Brenton," interrupted Ferris, "John Speed was a newspaper man, and he must ask strangers how they like the country. He has inquired so often while interviewing foreigners for his paper that now he cannot abandon his old phrase. Mr. Brenton has been with us but a short time," continued Ferris, "and so you know, Speed, you can hardly expect him to answer your inevitable question."

"What part of the country are you from?" asked Speed.

"Cincinnati," answered Brenton, feeling almost as if he were an American tourist doing the continent of Europe.

"Cincinnati, eh? Well, I congratulate you. I do not know any place in America that I would sooner die in, as they call it, than Cincinnati. You see, I am a Chicago man myself."

Brenton did not like the jocular familiarity of the newspaper man, and found himself rather astonished to learn that in the spirit-world there were likes and dislikes, just as on earth.

"Chicago is a very enterprising city," he said, in a non-committal way.

"Chicago, my dear sir," said Speed, earnestly, "is the city. You will see that Chicago is going to be the great city of the world before you are a hundred years older. By the way, Ferris," said the Chicago man, suddenly recollecting something, "I have got Sommers over here with me."

"Ah!" said Ferris; "doing him any good?"

"Well, precious little, as far as I can see."

"Perhaps it would interest Mr. Brenton to meet him," said Ferris. "I think, Brenton, you asked me a while ago if there was any hell here, or any punishment. Mr. Speed can show you a man in hell."

"Really?" asked Brenton.

"Yes," said Speed; "I think if ever a man was in misery, he is. The trouble with Sommers was this. He—well, he died of delirium tremens, and so, of course, you know what the matter was. Sommers had drunk Chicago whisky for thirty-five years straight along, and never added to it the additional horror of Chicago water. You see what his condition became, both physical and mental. Many people tried to reform Sommers, because he was really a brilliant man; but it was no use. Thirst had become a disease with him, and from the mental part of that disease, although his physical yearning is now gone of course, he suffers. Sommers would give his whole future for one glass of good old Kentucky whisky. He sees it on the counters, he sees men drink it, and he stands beside them in agony. That's why I brought him over here. I thought that he wouldn't see the colour of whisky as it sparkles in the glass; but now he is in the Café Quadra watching men drink. You may see him sitting there with all the agony of unsatisfied desire gleaming from his face."

"And what do you do with a man like that?" asked Brenton.

"Do? Well, to tell the truth, there is nothing to do. I took him away from Chicago, hoping to ease his trouble a little; but it has had no effect."

"It will come out all right by-and-by," said Ferris, who noticed the pained look on Brenton's face. "It is the period of probation that he has to pass through. It will wear off. He merely goes through the agonies he would have suffered on earth if he had suddenly been deprived of his favourite intoxicant."

"Well," said Speed, "you won't come with me, then? All right, good-bye. I hope to see you again, Mr. Brenton," and with that they separated.

Brenton spent two or three days in Venice, but all the time the old home hunger was upon him. He yearned for news of Cincinnati. He wanted to be back, and several times the wish brought him there, but he instantly returned. At last he said to Ferris—

"I am tired. I must go home. I have got to see how things are going."

"I wouldn't if I were you," replied Ferris.

"No, I know you wouldn't. Your temperament is indifferent. I would rather be miserable with knowledge than happy in ignorance. Good-bye."

It was evening when he found himself in Cincinnati. The weather was bright and clear, and apparently cold. Men's feet crisped on the frozen pavement, and the streets had that welcome, familiar look which they always have to the returned traveller when he reaches the city he calls his home. The newsboys were rushing through the streets yelling their papers at the top of their voices. He heard them, but paid little attention.

"All about the murder! Latest edition! All about the poison case!"

He felt that he must have a glimpse at a paper, and, entering the office of an hotel where a man was reading one, he glanced over his shoulder at the page before him, and was horror-stricken to see the words in startling headlines—

THE BRENTON MURDER.

The Autopsy shows that Morphine was the Poison used.

Enough found to have killed a Dozen Men.

Mrs. Brenton arrested for Committing the Horrible

Deed.

CHAPTER IV.

For a moment Brenton was so bewildered and amazed at the awful headlines which he read, that he could hardly realize what had taken place. The fact that he had been poisoned, although it gave him a strange sensation, did not claim his attention as much as might have been thought. Curiously enough he was more shocked at finding himself, as it were, the talk of the town, the central figure of a great newspaper sensation. But the thing that horrified him was the fact that his wife had been arrested for his murder. His first impulse was to go to her at once, but he next thought it better to read what the paper said about the matter, so as to become possessed of all the facts. The headlines, he said to himself, often exaggerated things, and there was a possibility that the body of the article would not bear out the naming announcement above it. But as he read on and on, the situation seemed to become more and more appalling. He saw that his friends had been suspicious of his sudden death, and had insisted on a post-mortem examination. That examination had been conducted by three of the most eminent physicians of Cincinnati, and the three doctors had practically agreed that the deceased, in the language of the verdict, had come to his death through morphia poisoning, and the coroner's jury had brought in a verdict that "the said William Brenton had been poisoned by some person unknown." Then the article went on to state how suspicion had gradually fastened itself upon his wife, and at last her arrest had been ordered. The arrest had taken place that day.

After reading this, Brenton was in an agony of mind. He pictured his dainty and beautiful wife in a stone cell in the city prison. He foresaw the horrors of the public trial, and the deep grief and pain which the newspaper comments on the case would cause to a woman educated and refined. Of course, Brenton had not the slightest doubt in his own mind about the result of the trial. His wife would be triumphantly acquitted; but, all the same, the terrible suspense which she must suffer in the meanwhile would not be compensated for by the final verdict of the jury.

Brenton at once went to the jail, and wandered through that gloomy building, searching for his wife. At last he found her, but it was in a very comfortable room in the sheriffs residence. The terror and the trials of the last few days had aged her perceptibly, and it cut Brenton to the heart to think that he stood there before her, and could not by any means say a soothing word that she would understand. That she had wept many bitter tears since the terrible Christmas morning was evident; there were dark circles under her beautiful eyes that told of sleepless nights. She sat in a comfortable armchair, facing the window; and looked steadily out at the dreary winter scene with eyes that apparently saw nothing. Her hands lay idly on her lap, and now and then she caught her breath in a way that was half a sob and half a gasp.

Presently the sheriff himself entered the room.

"Mrs. Brenton," he said, "there is a gentleman here who wishes to see you. Mr. Roland, he tells me his name is, an old friend of yours. Do you care to see any one?"

The lady turned her head slowly round, and looked at the sheriff for a moment, seemingly not understanding what he said. Finally she answered, dreamily—

"Roland? Oh, Stephen! Yes, I shall be very glad to see him. Ask him to come in, please."

The next moment Stephen Roland entered, and somehow the fact that he had come to console Mrs. Brenton did not at all please the invisible man who stood between them.

"My dear Mrs. Brenton," began Roland, "I hope you are feeling better to-day? Keep up your courage, and be brave. It is only for a very short time. I have retained the noted criminal lawyers, Benham and Brown, for the defence. You could not possibly have better men."

At the word "criminal" Mrs. Brenton shuddered.

"Alice," continued Roland, sitting down near her, and drawing his chair closer to her, "tell me that you will not lose your courage. I want you to be brave, for the sake of your friends."

He took her listless hand in his own, and she did not withdraw it.

Brenton felt passing over him the pangs of impotent rage, as he saw this act on the part of Roland.

Roland had been an unsuccessful suitor for the hand which he now held in his own, and Brenton thought it the worst possible taste, to say the least, that he should take advantage now of her terrible situation to ingratiate himself into her favour.

The nearest approach to a quarrel that Brenton and his wife had had during their short six months of wedded life was on the subject of the man who now held her hand in his own. It made Brenton impatient to think that a woman with all her boasted insight into character, her instincts as to what was right and what was wrong, had such little real intuition that she did not see into the character of the man whom they were discussing; but a woman never thinks it a crime for a man to have been in love with her, whatever opinion of that man her husband may hold.

"It is awful! awful! awful!" murmured the poor lady, as the tears again rose to her eyes.

"Of course it is," said Roland; "it is particularly awful that they should accuse you, of all persons in the world, of this so-called crime. For my part I do not believe that he was poisoned at all, but we will soon straighten things out. Benham and Brown will give up everything and devote their whole attention to this case until it is finished. Everything will be done that money or friends can do, and all that we ask is that you keep up your courage, and do not be downcast with the seeming awfulness of the situation."

Mrs. Brenton wept silently, but made no reply. It was evident, however, that she was consoled by the words and the presence of her visitor. Strange as it may appear, this fact enraged Brenton, although he had gone there for the very purpose of cheering and comforting his wife. All the bitterness he had felt before against his former rival was revived, and his rage was the more agonizing because it was inarticulate. Then there flashed over him Ferris's sinister advice to leave things alone in the world that he had left. He felt that he could stand this no longer, and the next instant he found himself again in the wintry streets of Cincinnati.

The name of the lawyers, Benham and Brown, kept repeating itself in his mind, and he resolved to go to their office and hear, if he could, what preparations were being made for the defence of a woman whom he knew to be innocent. He found, when he got to the office of these noted lawyers, that the two principals were locked in their private room; and going there, he found them discussing the case with the coolness and impersonal feeling that noted lawyers have even when speaking of issues that involve life or death.

"Yes," Benham was saying, "I think that, unless anything new turns up, that is the best line of defence we can adopt."

"What do you think might turn up?" asked Brown.

"Well, you can never tell in these cases. They may find something else—they may find the poison, for instance, or the package that contained it. Perhaps a druggist will remember having sold it to this woman, and then, of course, we shall have to change our plans. I need not say that it is strictly necessary in this case to give out no opinions whatever to newspaper men. The papers will be full of rumours, and it is just as well if we can keep our line of defence hidden until the time for action comes."

"Still," said Brown, who was the younger partner, "it is as well to keep in with the newspaper fellows; they'll be here as soon as they find we have taken charge of the defence."

"Well, I have no doubt you can deal with them in such a way as to give them something to write up, and yet not disclose anything we do not wish known."

"I think you can trust me to do that," said Brown, with a self-satisfied air.

"I shall leave that part of the matter entirely in your hands," replied Benham. "It is better not to duplicate or mix matters, and if any newspaper man comes to see me I will refer him to you. I will say I know nothing of the case whatever."

"Very well," answered Brown. "Now, between ourselves, what do you think of the case?"

"Oh, it will make a great sensation. I think it will probably be one of the most talked-of cases that we have ever been connected with."

"Yes, but what do you think of her guilt or innocence?"

"As to that," said Benham, calmly, "I haven't the slightest doubt. She murdered him."

As he said this, Brenton, forgetting himself for a moment, sprang forward as if to strangle the lawyer. The statement Benham had made seemed the most appalling piece of treachery. That men should take a woman's money for defending her, and actually engage in a case when they believed their client guilty, appeared to Brenton simply infamous.

"I agree with you," said Brown. "Of course she was the only one to benefit by his death. The simple fool willed everything to her, and she knew it; and his doing so is the more astounding when you remember he was quite well aware that she had a former lover whom she would gladly have married if he had been as rich as Brenton. The supreme idiocy of some men as far as their wives are concerned is something awful."

"Yes," answered Benham, "it is. But I tell you, Brown, she is no ordinary woman. The very conception of that murder had a stroke of originality about it that I very much admire. I do not remember anything like it in the annals of crime. It is the true way in which a murder should be committed. The very publicity of the occasion was a safeguard. Think of poisoning a man at a dinner that he has given himself, in the midst of a score of friends. I tell you that there was a dash of bravery about it that commands my admiration."

"Do you imagine Roland had anything to do with it?"

"Well, I had my doubts about that at first, but I think he is innocent, although from what I know of the man he will not hesitate to share the proceeds of the crime. You mark my words, they will be married within a year from now if she is acquitted. I believe Roland knows her to be guilty."

"I thought as much," said Brown, "by his actions here, and by some remarks he let drop. Anyhow, our credit in the affair will be all the greater if we succeed in getting her off. Yes," he continued, rising and pushing back his chair, "Madam Brenton is a murderess."

CHAPTER V.

Brenton found himself once more in the streets of Cincinnati, in a state of mind that can hardly be described. Rage and grief struggled for the mastery, and added to the tumult of these passions was the uncertainty as to what he should do, or what he could do. He could hardly ask the advice of Ferris again, for his whole trouble arose from his neglect of the counsel that gentleman had already given him. In his new sphere he did not know where to turn. He found himself wondering whether in the spirit-land there was any firm of lawyers who could advise him, and he remembered then how singularly ignorant he was regarding the conditions of existence in the world to which he now belonged. However, he felt that he must consult with somebody, and Ferris was the only one to whom he could turn. A moment later he was face to face with him.

"Mr. Ferris," he said, "I am in the most grievous trouble, and I come to you in the hope that, if you cannot help me, you can at least advise me what to do."

"If your trouble has come," answered Ferris, with a shade of irony in his voice, "through following the advice that I have already given you, I shall endeavour, as well as I am able, to help you out of it."

"You know very well," cried Brenton, hotly, "that my whole trouble has occurred through neglecting your advice, or, at least, through deliberately not following it. I could not follow it."

"Very well, then," said Ferris, "I am not surprised that you are in a difficulty. You must remember that such a crisis is an old story with us here."

"But, my dear sir," said Brenton, "look at the appalling condition of things, the knowledge of which has just come to me. It seems I was poisoned, but of course that doesn't matter. I feel no resentment against the wretch who did it. But the terrible thing is that my wife has been arrested for the crime, and I have just learned that her own lawyers actually believe her guilty."

"That fact," said Ferris, calmly, "will not interfere with their eloquent pleading when the case comes to trial."

Brenton glared at the man who was taking things so coolly, and who proved himself so unsympathetic; but an instant after he realized the futility of quarrelling with the only person who could give him advice, so he continued, with what patience he could command—

"The situation is this: My wife has been arrested for the crime of murdering me. She is now in the custody of the sheriff. Her trouble and anxiety of mind are fearful to contemplate."

"My dear sir," said Ferris, "there is no reason why you or anybody else should contemplate it."

"How can you talk in that cold-blooded way?" cried Brenton, indignantly. "Could you see your wife, or any one you held dear, incarcerated for a dreadful crime, and yet remain calm and collected, as you now appear to be when you hear of another's misfortune?"

"My dear fellow," said Ferris, "of course it is not to be expected that one who has had so little experience with this existence should have any sense of proportion. You appear to be speaking quite seriously. You do not seem at all to comprehend the utter triviality of all this."

"Good gracious!" cried Brenton, "do you call it a trivial thing that a woman is in danger of her life for a crime which she never committed?"

"If she is innocent," said the other, in no way moved by the indignation of his comrade, "surely that state of things will be brought out in the courts, and no great harm will be done, even looking at things from the standpoint of the world you have left. But I want you to get into the habit of looking at things from the standpoint of this world, and not of the other. Suppose that what you would call the worst should happen—suppose she is hanged—what then?"

Brenton stood simply speechless with indignation at this brutal remark.

"If you will just look at things correctly," continued Ferris, imperturbably, "you will see that there is probably a moment of anguish, perhaps not even that moment, and then your wife is here with you in the land of spirits. I am sure that is a consummation devoutly to be wished. Even a man in your state of mind must see the reasonableness of this. Now, looking at the question in what you would call its most serious aspect, see how little it amounts to. It isn't worth a moment's thought, whichever way it goes."

"You think nothing, then, of the disgrace of such a death—of the bitter injustice of it?"

"When you were in the world did you ever see a child cry over a broken toy? Did the sight pain you to any extent? Did you not know that a new toy could be purchased that would quite obliterate all thoughts of the other? Did the simple griefs of childhood carry any deep and lasting consternation to the mind of a grown-up man? Of course it did not. You are sensible enough to know that. Well, we here in this world look on the pain and struggles and trials of people in the world you have left, just as an aged man looks on the tribulations of children over a broken doll. That is all it really amounts to. That is what I mean when I say that you have not yet got your sense of proportion. Any grief and misery there is in the world you have left is of such an ephemeral, transient nature, that when we think for a moment of the free, untrammelled, and painless life there is beyond, those petty troubles sink into insignificance. My dear fellow, be sensible, take my advice. I have really a strong interest in you, and I advise you, entirely for your own welfare, to forget all about it. Very soon you will have something much more important to do than lingering around the world you have left. If your wife comes amongst us I am sure you will be glad to welcome her, and to teach her the things that you will have already found out of your new life. If she does not appear, then you will know that, even from the old-world standpoint, things have gone what you would call 'all right.' Let these trivial matters go, and attend to the vastly more important concerns that will soon engage your attention here."

Ferris talked earnestly, and it was evident, even to Brenton, that he meant what he said. It was hard to find a pretext for a quarrel with a man at once so calm and so perfectly sure of himself.

"We will not talk any more about it," said Brenton. "I presume people here agree to differ, just as they did in the world we have both left."

"Certainly, certainly," answered Ferris. "Of course, you have just heard my opinion; but you will find myriads of others who do not share it with me. You will meet a great many who are interested in the subject of communication with the world they have left. You will, of course, excuse me when I say that I consider such endeavours not worth talking about."

"Do you know any one who is interested in that sort of thing? and can you give me an introduction to him?"

"Oh! for that matter," said Ferris, "you have had an introduction to one of the most enthusiastic investigators of the subject. I refer to Mr. John Speed, late of Chicago."

"Ah!" said Brenton, rather dubiously. "I must confess that I was not very favourably impressed with Mr. Speed. Probably I did him an injustice."

"You certainly did," said Ferris. "You will find Speed a man well worth knowing, even if he does waste himself on such futile projects as a scheme for communicating with a community so evanescent as that of Chicago. You will like Speed better the more you know him. He really is very philanthropic, and has Sommers on his hands just now. From what he said after you left Venice, I imagine he does not entertain the same feeling toward you as you do toward him. I would see Speed if I were you."

"I will think about it," said Brenton, as they separated.

To know that a man thinks well of a person is no detriment to further acquaintance with that man, even if the first impressions have not been favourable; and after Ferris told Brenton that Speed had thought well of him, Brenton found less difficulty in seeking the Chicago enthusiast.

"I have been in a good deal of trouble," Brenton said to Speed, "and have been talking to Ferris about it. I regret to say that he gave me very little encouragement, and did not seem at all to appreciate my feelings in the matter."

"Oh, you mustn't mind Ferris," said Speed. "He is a first-rate fellow, but he is as cold and unsympathetic as—well, suppose we say as an oyster. His great hobby is non-intercourse with the world we have left. Now, in that I don't agree with him, and there are thousands who don't agree with him. I admit that there are cases where a man is more unhappy if he frequents the old world than he would be if he left it alone. But then there are other cases where just the reverse is true. Take my own experience, for example; I take a peculiar pleasure in rambling around Chicago. I admit that it is a grievance to me, as an old newspaper man, to see the number of scoops I could have on my esteemed contemporaries, but—"

"Scoop? What is that?" asked Brenton, mystified.

"Why, a scoop is a beat, you know."

"Yes, but I don't know. What is a beat?"

"A beat or a scoop, my dear fellow, is the getting of a piece of news that your contemporary does not obtain. You never were in the newspaper business? Well, sir, you missed it. Greatest business in the world. You know everything that is going on long before anybody else does, and the way you can reward your friends and jump with both feet on your enemies is one of the delights of existence down there."

"Well, what I wanted to ask you was this," said Brenton. "You have made a speciality of finding out whether there could be any communication between one of us, for instance, and one who is an inhabitant of the other world. Is such communication possible?"

"I have certainly devoted some time to it, but I can't say that my success has been flattering. My efforts have been mostly in the line of news. I have come on some startling information which my facilities here gave me access to, and I confess I have tried my best to put some of the boys on to it. But there is a link loose somewhere. Now, what is your trouble? Do you want to get a message to anybody?"

"My trouble is this," said Brenton, briefly, "I am here because a few days ago I was poisoned."

"George Washington!" cried the other, "you don't say so! Have the

113

newspapers got on to the fact?"

"I regret to say that they have."

"What an item that would have been if one paper had got hold of it and the others hadn't! I suppose they all got on to it at the same time?"

"About that," said Brenton, "I don't know, and I must confess that I do not care very much. But here is the trouble—my wife has been arrested for my murder, and she is as innocent as I am."

"Sure of that?"

"Sure of it?" cried the other indignantly. "Of course I am sure of it."

"Then who is the guilty person?"

"Ah, that," said Brenton, "I do not yet know."

"Then how can you be sure she is not guilty?"

"If you talk like that," exclaimed Brenton, "I have nothing more to say."

"Now, don't get offended, I beg of you. I am merely looking at this from a newspaper standpoint, you know. You must remember it is not you who will decide the matter, but a jury of your very stupid fellow-countrymen. Now, you can never tell what a jury will do, except that it will do something idiotic. Therefore, it seems to me that the very first step to be taken is to find out who the guilty party is. Don't you see the force of that?"

"Yes, I do."

"Very well, then. Now, what were the circumstances of this crime? who was to profit by your death?"

Brenton winced at this.

"I see how it is," said the other, "and I understand why you don't answer. Now—you'll excuse me if I am frank—your wife was the one who benefited most by your death, was she not?"

"No," cried the other indignantly, "she was not the one. That is what the lawyers said. Why in the world should she want to poison me, when she had all my wealth at her command as it was?"

"Yes, that's a strong point," said Speed. "You were a reasonably good husband, I suppose? Rather generous with the cash?"

"Generous?" cried the other. "My wife always had everything she wanted."

"Ah, well, there was no—you'll excuse me, I am sure—no former lover in the case, was there?"

Again Brenton winced, and he thought of Roland sitting beside his wife with her hand in his.

"I see," said Speed; "you needn't answer. Now what were the circumstances, again?"

"They were these: At a dinner which I gave, where some twenty or twenty-five of my friends were assembled, poison, it appears, was put into my cup of coffee. That is all I know of it."

"Who poured out that cup of coffee?"

"My wife did."

"Ah! Now, I don't for a moment say she is guilty, remember; but you must admit that, to a stupid jury, the case might look rather bad against her."

"Well, granted that it does, there is all the more need that I should come to her assistance if possible."

"Certainly, certainly!" said Speed. "Now, I'll tell you what we have to do. We must get, if possible, one of the very brightest Chicago reporters on the track of this thing, and we have to get him on the track of it early. Come with me to Chicago. We will try an experiment, and I am sure you will lend your mind entirely to the effort. We must act in conjunction in this affair, and you are just the man I've been wanting, some one who is earnest and who has something at stake in the matter. We may fail entirely, but I think it's worth the trying. Will you come?"

"Certainly," said Brenton; "and I cannot tell you how much I appreciate your interest and sympathy."

Arriving at a brown stone building on the corner of two of the principal streets in Chicago, Brenton and Speed ascended quickly to one of the top floors. It was nearly midnight, and two upper stories of the huge dark building were brilliantly lighted, as was shown on the outside by the long rows of glittering windows. They entered a room where a man was seated at a table, with coat and vest thrown off, and his hat set well back on his head. Cold as it was outside, it was warm in this man's room, and the room was blue with smoke. A black corn-cob pipe was in his teeth, and the man was writing away as if for dear life, on sheets of coarse white copy paper, stopping now and then to fill up his pipe or to relight it after it had gone out.

"There," said Speed, waving his hand towards the writer with a certain air of proprietary pride, "there sits one of the very cleverest men on the Chicago press. That fellow, sir, is gifted with a nose for news which has no equal in America. He will ferret out a case that he once starts on with an unerringness that would charm you. Yes, sir, I got him his present situation on this paper, and I can tell you it was a good one."

"He must have been a warm friend of yours?" said Brenton, indifferently, as if he did not take much interest in the eulogy.

"Quite the contrary," said Speed. "He was a warm enemy, made it mighty warm for me sometimes. He was on an opposition paper, but I tell you, although I was no chicken in newspaper business, that man would scoop the daylight out of me any time he tried. So, to get rid of opposition, I got the managing editor to appoint him to a place on our paper; and I tell you, he has never regretted it. Yes, sir, there sits George Stratton, a man who knows his business. Now," he said, "let us concentrate our attention on him. First let us see whether, by putting our whole minds to it, we can make any impression on his mind whatever. You see how busily he is engaged. He is thoroughly absorbed in his work. That is George all over. Whatever his assignment is, George throws himself right into it, and thinks of nothing else until it is finished. Now then."

In that dingy, well-lighted room George Stratton sat busily pencilling out the lines that were to appear in next morning's paper. He was evidently very much engrossed in his task, as Speed had said. If he had looked about him, which he did not, he would have said that he was entirely alone. All at once his attention seemed to waver, and he passed his hand over his brow, while perplexity came into his face. Then he noticed that his pipe was out, and, knocking the ashes from it by rapping the bowl on the side of the table, he filled it with an absent-mindedness unusual with him. Again he turned to his writing, and again he passed his hand over his brow. Suddenly, without any apparent cause, he looked first to the right and then to the left of him. Once more he tried to write, but, noticing his pipe was out, he struck another match and nervously puffed away, until clouds of blue smoke rose around him. There was a look of annoyance and perplexity in his face as he bent resolutely to his writing. The door opened, and a man appeared on the threshold.

"Anything more about the convention, George?" he said.

"Yes; I am just finishing this. Sort of pen pictures, you know."

"Perhaps you can let me have what you have done. I'll fix it up."

"All right," said Stratton, bunching up the manuscript in front of him, and handing it to the city editor.

That functionary looked at the number of pages, and then at the writer.

"Much more of this, George?" he said. "We'll be a little short of room in the morning, you know."

"Well," said the other, sitting back in his chair, "it is pretty good stuff that. Folks always like the pen pictures of men engaged in the skirmish better than the reports of what most of them say."

"Yes," said the city editor, "that's so."

"Still," said Stratton, "we could cut it off at the last page. Just let me see the last two pages, will you?"

These were handed to him, and, running his eye through them, he drew his knife across one of the pages, and put at the bottom the cabalistic mark which indicated the end of the copy.

"There! I think I will let it go at that. Old Rickenbeck don't amount to much, anyhow. We'll let him go."

"All right," said the city editor. "I think we won't want anything more to-night."

Stratton put his hands behind his head, with his fingers interlaced, and leaned back in his chair, placing his heels upon the table before him. A thought-reader, looking at his face, could almost have followed the theme that occupied his mind. Suddenly bringing his feet down with a crash to the floor, he rose and went into the city editor's room.

"See here," he said. "Have you looked into that Cincinnati case at all?"

"What Cincinnati case?" asked the local editor, looking up.

"Why, that woman who is up for poisoning her husband."

"Oh yes; we had something of it in the despatches this morning. It's rather out of the local line, you know."

"Yes, I know it is. But it isn't out of the paper's line. I tell you that case is going to make a sensation. She's pretty as a picture. Been married only six months, and it seems to be a dead sure thing that she poisoned her husband. That trial's going to make racy reading, especially if they bring in a verdict of guilty."

The city editor looked interested.

"Want to go down there, George?"

"Well, do you know, I think it'll pay."

"Let me see, this is the last day of the convention, isn't it? And Clark comes back from his vacation to-morrow. Well, if you think it's worth it, take a trip down there, and look the ground over, and give us a special article that we can use on the first day of the trial."

118

"I'll do it," said George.

Speed looked at Brenton.

"What would old Ferris say now, eh?"

CHAPTER VI.

Next morning George Stratton was on the railway train speeding towards Cincinnati. As he handed to the conductor his mileage book, he did not say to him, lightly transposing the old couplet—

"Here, railroad man, take thrice thy fee,

For spirits twain do ride with me."

George Stratton was a practical man, and knew nothing of spirits, except those which were in a small flask in his natty little valise.

When he reached Cincinnati, he made straight for the residence of the sheriff. He felt that his first duty was to become friends with such an important official. Besides this, he wished to have an interview with the prisoner. He had arranged in his mind, on the way there, just how he would write a preliminary article that would whet the appetite of the readers of the Chicago Argus for any further developments that might occur during and after the trial. He would write the whole thing in the form of a story.

First, there would be a sketch of the life of Mrs. Brenton and her husband. This would be number one, and above it would be the Roman numeral I. Under the heading II. would be a history of the crime. Under III. what had occurred afterwards—the incidents that had led suspicion towards the unfortunate woman, and that sort of thing. Under the numeral IV. would be his interview with the prisoner, if he were fortunate enough to get one. Under V. he would give the general opinion of Cincinnati on the crime, and on the guilt or innocence of Mrs. Brenton. This article he already saw in his mind's eye occupying nearly half a page of the Argus. All would be in leaded type, and written in a style and manner that would attract attention, for he felt that he was first on the ground, and would not have the usual rush in preparing his copy which had been the bane of his life. It would give the Argus practically the lead in this case, which he was convinced would become one of national importance.

The sheriff received him courteously, and, looking at the card he presented, saw the name Chicago Argus in the corner. Then he stood visibly on his guard—an attitude assumed by all wise officials when they find themselves brought face to face with a newspaper man; for they know, however carefully an article may be prepared, it will likely contain some unfortunate overlooked phrase which may have a damaging effect in a future political campaign.

"I wanted to see you," began Stratton, coming straight to the point, "in reference to the Brenton murder."

"I may say at once," replied the sheriff, "that if you wish an interview with the prisoner, it is utterly impossible, because her lawyers, Benham and Brown, have positively forbidden her to see a newspaper man."

"That shows," said Stratton, "they are wise men who understand their business. Nevertheless, I wish to have an interview with Mrs. Brenton. But what I wanted to say to you is this: I believe the case will be very much talked about, and that before many weeks are over. Of course you know the standing the Argus has in newspaper circles. What it says will have an influence, even over the Cincinnati press. I think you will admit that. Now a great many newspaper men consider an official their natural enemy. I do not; at least, I do not until I am forced to. Any reference that I may make to you I am more than willing to submit to you before it goes to Chicago. I will give you my word, if you want it, that nothing will be said referring to your official position, or to yourself personally, that you do not see before it appears in print. Of course you will be up for re-election. I never met a sheriff who wasn't."

The sheriff smiled at this, and did not deny it.

"Very well. Now, I may tell you my belief is that this case is going to have a powerful influence on your re-election. Here is a young and pretty woman who is to be tried for a terrible crime. Whether she is guilty or innocent, public sympathy is going to be with her. If I were in your place, I would prefer to be known as her friend rather than as her enemy."

"My dear sir," said the sheriff, "my official position puts me in the attitude of neither friend nor enemy of the unfortunate woman. I have simply a certain duty to do, and that duty I intend to perform."

"Oh, that's all right!" exclaimed the newspaper man, jauntily. "I, for one, am not going to ask you to take a step outside your duties; but an official may do his duty, and yet, at the same time, do a friendly act for a newspaper man, or even for a prisoner. In the language of the old chestnut, 'If you don't help me, don't help the bear.' That's all I ask."

"You maybe sure, Mr. Stratton, that anything I can do to help you I shall be glad to do; and now let me give you a hint. If you want to see Mrs. Brenton, the best thing is to get permission from her lawyers. If I were you I would not see Benham—he's rather a hard nut, Benham is, although you needn't tell him I said so. You get on the right side of Brown. Brown has some political aspirations himself, and he does not want to offend a man on so powerful a paper as the Argus, even if it is not a Cincinnati paper. Now, if you make him the same offer you have made to me, I think it will be all right. If he sees your copy before it goes into print, and if you keep your word with him that nothing will appear that he does not see, I think you will succeed in getting an interview with Mrs. Brenton. If you bring me a note from Brown, I shall be very glad to allow you to see her."

Stratton thanked the sheriff for his hint. He took down in his note-book the address of the lawyers, and the name especially of Mr. Brown. The two men shook hands, and Stratton felt that they understood each other.

When Mr. Stratton was ushered into the private office of Brown, and handed that gentleman his card, he noticed the lawyer perceptibly freeze over.

"Ahem," said the legal gentleman; "you will excuse me if I say that my time is rather precious. Did you wish to see me professionally?"

"Yes," replied Stratton, "that is, from a newspaper standpoint of the profession."

"Ah," said the other, "in reference to what?"

"To the Brenton case."

"Well, my dear sir, I have had, very reluctantly, to refuse information that I would have been happy to give, if I could, to our own newspaper men; and so I may say to you at once that I scarcely think it will be possible for me to be of any service to an outside paper like the Argus"

"Local newspaper men," said Stratton, "represent local fame. That you already possess. I represent national fame, which, if you will excuse my saying so, you do not yet possess. The fact that I am in Cincinnati to-day, instead of in Chicago, shows what we Chicago people think of the Cincinnati case. I believe, and the Argus believes, that this case is going to be one of national importance. Now, let me ask you one question. Will you state frankly what your objection is to having a newspaper man, for instance, interview Mrs. Brenton, or get any information relating to this case from her or others whom you have the power of controlling?"

"I shall answer that question," said Brown, "as frankly as you put it. You are a man of the world, and know, of course, that we are all selfish, and in business matters look entirely after our own interests. My interest in this case is to defend my client. Your interest in this case is to make a sensational article. You want to get facts if possible, but, in any event, you want to write up a readable column or two for your paper. Now, if I allowed you to see Mrs. Brenton, she might say something to you, and you might publish it, that would not only endanger her chances, but would seriously embarrass us, as her lawyers, in our defence of the case."

"You have stated the objection very plainly and forcibly," said Stratton, with a look of admiration, as if the powerful arguments of the lawyer had had a great effect on him. "Now, if I understand your argument, it simply amounts to this, that you would have no objection to my interviewing Mrs. Brenton if you have the privilege of editing the copy. In other words, if nothing were printed but what you approve of, you would not have the slightest hesitancy about allowing me that interview."

"No, I don't know that I would," admitted the lawyer.

"Very well, then. Here is my proposition to you: I am here to look after the interests of our paper in this particular case. The Argus is probably going to be the first paper outside of Cincinnati that will devote a large amount of space to the Brenton trial, in addition to what is received from the Associated Press dispatches. Now you can give me a great many facilities in this matter if you care to do so, and in return I am perfectly willing to submit to you every line of copy that concerns you or your client before it is sent, and I give you my word of honour that nothing shall appear but what you have seen and approved of. If you want to cut out something that I think is vitally important, then I shall tell you frankly that I intend to print it, but will modify it as much as I possibly can to suit your views."

"I see," said the lawyer. "In other words, as you have just remarked, I am to give you special facilities in this matter, and then, when you find out some fact which I wish kept secret, and which you have obtained because of the facilities I have given to you, you will quite frankly tell me that it must go in, and then, of course, I shall be helpless except to debar you from any further facilities, as you call them. No, sir, I do not care to make any such bargain."

"Well, suppose I strike out that clause of agreement, and say to you that I will send nothing but what you approve of, would you then write me a note to the sheriff and allow me to see the prisoner?"

"I am sorry to say"—the lawyer hesitated for a moment, and glanced at the card, then added—"Mr. Stratton, that I do not see my way clear to granting your request."

"I think," said Stratton, rising, "that you are doing yourself an injustice. You are refusing—I may as well tell you first as last—what is a great privilege. Now, you have had some experience in your business, and I have had some experience in mine, and I beg to inform you that men who are much more prominent in the history of their country than any one I can at present think of in Cincinnati, have tried to balk me in the pursuit of my business, and have failed."

"In that matter, of course," said Brown, "I must take my chances. I don't see the use of prolonging this interview. As you have been so frank as to—I won't say threaten, perhaps warn is the better word—as you have been so good as to warn me, I may, before we part, just give you a word of caution. Of course we, in Cincinnati, are perfectly willing to admit that Chicago people are the smartest on earth, but I may say that if you print a word in your paper which is untrue and which is damaging to our side of the case, or if you use any methods that are unlawful in obtaining the information you so much desire, you will certainly get your paper into trouble, and you will run some little personal risk yourself."

"Well, as you remarked a moment ago, Mr. Brown, I shall have to take the chances of that. I am here to get the news, and if I don't succeed it will be the first time in my life."

"Very well, sir," said the lawyer. "I wish you good evening."

"Just one thing more," said the newspaper man, "before I leave you."

"My dear sir," said the lawyer, impatiently, "I am very busy. I've already given you a liberal share of my time. I must request that this interview end at once."

"I thought," said Mr. Stratton, calmly, "that perhaps you might be interested in the first article that I am going to write. I shall devote one column in the Argus of the day after to-morrow to your defence of the case, and whether your theory of defence is a tenable one or not."

Mr. Brown pushed back his chair and looked earnestly at the young man. That individual was imperturbably pulling on his gloves, and at the moment was buttoning one of them.

"Our defence!" cried the lawyer. "What do you know of our defence?"

"My dear sir," said Stratton, "I know all about it."

"Sir, that is impossible. Nobody knows what our defence is to be except Mr. Benham and myself."

"And Mr. Stratton, of the Chicago Argus," replied the young man, as he buttoned his coat.

"May I ask, then, what the defence is?"

"Certainly," answered the Chicago man. "Your defence is that Mr.

125

Brenton was insane, and that he committed suicide."

Even Mr. Brown's habitual self-control, acquired by long years of training in keeping his feelings out of sight, for the moment deserted him. He drew his breath sharply, and cast a piercing glance at the young man before him, who was critically watching the lawyer's countenance, although he appeared to be entirely absorbed in buttoning his overcoat. Then Mr. Brown gave a short, dry laugh.

"I have met a bluff before," he said carelessly; "but I should like to know what makes you think that such is our defence?"

"Think!" cried the young man. "I don't think at all; I know it."

"How do you know it?"

"Well, for one thing, I know it by your own actions a moment ago. What first gave me an inkling of your defence was that book which is on your table. It is Forbes Winslow on the mind and the brain; a very interesting book, Mr. Brown, very interesting indeed. It treats of suicide, and the causes and conditions of the brain that will lead up to it. It is a very good book, indeed, to study in such a case. Good evening, Mr. Brown. I am sorry that we cannot co-operate in this matter."

Stratton turned and walked toward the door, while the lawyer gazed after him with a look of helpless astonishment on his face. As Stratton placed his hand on the door knob, the lawyer seemed to wake up as from a dream.

"Stop!" he cried; "I will give you a letter that will admit you to Mrs. Brenton."

CHAPTER VII.

"There!" said Speed to Brenton, triumphantly, "what do you think of that? Didn't I say George Stratton was the brightest newspaper man in Chicago? I tell you, his getting that letter from old Brown was one of the cleverest bits of diplomacy I ever saw. There you had quickness of perception, and nerve. All the time he was talking to old Brown he was just taking that man's measure. See how coolly he acted while he was drawing on his gloves and buttoning his coat as if ready to leave. Flung that at Brown all of a sudden as quiet as if he was saying nothing at all unusual, and all the time watching Brown out of the tail of his eye. Well, sir, I must admit, that although I have known George Stratton for years, I thought he was dished by that Cincinnati lawyer. I thought that George was just gracefully covering up his defeat, and there he upset old Brown's apple-cart in the twinkling of an eye. Now, you see the effect of all this. Brown has practically admitted to him what the line of defence is. Stratton won't publish it, of course; he has promised not to, but you see he can hold that over Brown's head, and get everything he wants unless they change their defence."

"Yes," remarked Brenton, slowly, "he seems to be a very sharp newspaper man indeed; but I don't like the idea of his going to interview my wife."

"Why, what is there wrong about that?"

"Well, there is this wrong about it—that she in her depression may say something that will tell against her."

"Even if she does, what of it? Isn't the lawyer going to see the letter before it is sent to the paper?"

"I am not so sure about that. Do you think Stratton will show the article to Brown if he gets what you call a scoop or a beat?"

"Why, of course he will," answered Speed, indignantly; "hasn't he given him his word that he will?"

"Yes, I know he has," said Brenton, dubiously; "but he is a newspaper man."

"Certainly he is," answered Speed, with strong emphasis; "that is the reason he will keep his word."

"I hope so, I hope so; but I must admit that the more I know you newspaper men, the more I see the great temptation you are under to preserve if possible the sensational features of an article."

"I'll bet you a drink—no, we can't do that," corrected Speed; "but you shall see that, if Brown acts square with Stratton, he will keep his word to the very letter with Brown. There is no use in our talking about the matter here. Let us follow Stratton, and see what comes of the interview."

"I think I prefer to go alone," said Brenton, coldly.

"Oh, as you like, as you like," answered the other, shortly. "I thought you wanted my help in this affair; but if you don't, I am sure I shan't intrude."

"That's all right," said Brenton; "come along. By the way, Speed, what do you think of that line of defence?"

"Well, I don't know enough of the circumstances of the case to know what to think of it. It seems to me rather a good line."

"It can't be a good line when it is not true. It is certain to break down."

"That's so," said Speed; "but I'll bet you four dollars and a half that they'll prove you a raving maniac before they are through with you. They'll show very likely that you tried to poison yourself two or three times; bring on a dozen of your friends to prove that they knew all your life you were insane."

"Do you think they will?" asked Brenton, uneasily.

"Think it? Why, I am sure of it. You'll go down to posterity as one of the most complete lunatics that ever, lived in Cincinnati. Oh, there won't be anything left of you when they get through with you."

Meanwhile, Stratton was making his way to the residence of the sheriff.

"Ah," said that official, when they met, "you got your letter, did you? Well, I thought you would."

"If you had heard the conversation between my estimable friend Mr. Brown and myself, up to the very last moment, you wouldn't have thought it."

"Well, Brown is generally very courteous towards newspaper men, and that's one reason you see his name in the papers a great deal."

"If I were a Cincinnati newspaper man, I can assure you that his name wouldn't appear very much in the columns of my paper."

"I am sorry to hear you say that. I thought Brown was very popular with the newspaper men. You got the letter, though, did you?"

"Yes; I got it. Here it is. Read it."

The sheriff scanned the brief note over, and put it in his pocket.

"Just take a chair for a moment, will you, and I will see if Mrs. Brenton is ready to receive you."

Stratton seated himself, and, pulling a paper from his pocket, was busily reading when the sheriff again entered.

"I am sorry to say," he began, "after you have had all this trouble, that Mrs. Brenton positively refuses to see you. You know I cannot compel a prisoner to meet any one. You understand that, of course."

"Perfectly," said Stratton, thinking for a moment. "See here, sheriff, I have simply got to have a talk with that woman. Now, can't you tell her I knew her husband, or something of that sort? I'll make it all right when I see her."

"The scoundrel!" said Brenton to Speed, as Stratton made this remark.

"My dear sir," said Speed, "don't you see he is just the man we want? This is not the time to be particular."

"Yes, but think of the treachery and meanness of telling a poor unfortunate woman that he was acquainted with her husband, who is only a few days dead."

"Now, see here," said Speed, "if you are going to look on matters in this way you will be a hindrance and not a help in the affair. Don't you appreciate the situation? Why, Mrs. Brenton's own lawyers, as you have said, think her guilty. What, then, can they learn by talking with her, or what good can they do her with their minds already prejudiced against her? Don't you see that?"

Brenton made no answer to this, but it was evident he was very ill at ease.

"Did you know her husband?" asked the sheriff.

"No, to tell you the truth, I never heard of him before. But I must see this lady, both for my good and hers, and I am not going to let a little thing like that stand between us. Won't you tell her that I have come with a letter from her own lawyers? Just show her the letter, and say that I will take up but very little of her time. I am sorry to ask this much of you, but you see how I am placed."

"Oh, that's all right," said the sheriff, good-naturedly; "I shall be very glad to do what you wish," and with that he once more disappeared.

The sheriff stayed away longer this time, and Stratton paced the room impatiently. Finally, the official returned, and said—

"Mrs. Brenton has consented to see you. Come this way, please. You will excuse me, I know," continued the sheriff, as they walked along together, "but it is part of my duty to remain in the room while you are talking with Mrs. Brenton."

"Certainly, certainly," said Stratton; "I understand that."

"Very well; then, if I may make a suggestion, I would say this: you should be prepared to ask just what you want to know, and do it all as speedily as possible, for really Mrs. Brenton is in a condition of nervous exhaustion that renders it almost cruel to put her through any rigid cross-examination."

"I understand that also," said Stratton; "but you must remember that she has a very much harder trial to undergo in the future. I am exceedingly anxious to get at the truth of this thing, and so, if it seems to you that I am asking a lot of very unnecessary questions, I hope you will not interfere with me as long as Mrs. Brenton consents to answer."

"I shall not interfere at all," said the sheriff; "I only wanted to caution you, for the lady may break down at any moment. If you can marshal your questions so that the most important ones come first, I think it will be wise. I presume you have them pretty well arranged in your own mind?"

"Well, I can't say that I have; you see, I am entirely in the dark. I got no help whatever from the lawyers, and from what I know of their defence I am thoroughly convinced that they are on the wrong track."

"What! did Brown say anything about the defence? That is not like his usual caution."

"He didn't intend to," answered Stratton; "but I found out all I wanted to know, nevertheless. You see, I shall have to ask what appears to be a lot of rambling, inconsequential questions because you can never tell in a case like this when you may get the key to the whole mystery."

"Well, here we are," said the sheriff, as he knocked at a door, and then pushed it open.

From the moment George Stratton saw Mrs. Brenton his interest in the case ceased to be purely journalistic.

Mrs. Brenton was standing near the window, and she appeared to be very calm and collected, but her fingers twitched nervously, clasping and unclasping each other. Her modest dress of black was certainly a very becoming one.

George thought he had never seen a woman so beautiful.

As she was standing up, she evidently intended the interview to be a short one.

"Madam," said Stratton, "I am very sorry indeed to trouble you; but

I have taken a great interest in the solution of this mystery, and I have your lawyers' permission to visit you. I assure you, anything you say will be submitted to them, so that there will be no danger of your case being prejudiced by any statements made."

"I am not afraid," said Mrs. Brenton, "that the truth will injure or prejudice my case."

"I am sure of that," answered the newspaper man; and then, knowing that she would not sit down if he asked her to, he continued diplomatically, "Madam, will you permit me to sit down? I wish to write out my notes as carefully as possible. Accuracy is my strong point."

"Certainly," said Mrs. Brenton; and, seeing that it was not probable the interview would be a short one, she seated herself by the window, while the sheriff took a chair in the corner, and drew a newspaper from his pocket.

"Now, madam," said the special, "a great number of the questions I ask you may seem trivial, but as I said to the sheriff a moment ago, some word of yours that appears to you entirely unconnected with the case may give me a clue which will be exceedingly valuable. You will, therefore, I am sure, pardon me if some of the questions I ask you appear irrelevant."

Mrs. Brenton bowed her head, but said nothing.

"Were your husband's business affairs in good condition at the time of his death?"

"As far as I know they were."

"Did you ever see anything in your husband's actions that would lead you to think him a man who might have contemplated suicide?"

Mrs. Brenton looked up with wide-open eyes.

"Certainly not," she said.

"Had he ever spoken to you on the subject of suicide?"

"I do not remember that he ever did."

"Was he ever queer in his actions? In short, did you ever notice anything about him that would lead you to doubt his sanity? I am sorry if questions I ask you seem painful, but I have reasons for wishing to be certain on this point."

"No," said Mrs. Brenton; "he was perfectly sane. No man could have been more so. I am certain that he never thought of committing suicide."

"Why are you so certain on that point?"

"I do not know why. I only know I am positive of it."

"Do you know if he had any enemy who might wish his death?"

"I doubt if he had an enemy in the world. I do not know of any."

"Have you ever heard him speak of anybody in a spirit of enmity?"

"Never. He was not a man who bore enmity against people. Persons whom he did not like he avoided."

"The poison, it is said, was put into his cup of coffee. Do you happen to know," said Stratton, turning to the sheriff, "how they came to that conclusion?"

"No, I do not," answered the sheriff. "In fact, I don't see any reason why they should think so."

"Was morphia found in the coffee cup afterwards?"

"No; at the time of the inquest all the things had been cleared away. I think it was merely presumed that the morphine was put into his coffee."

"Who poured out the coffee he drank that night?"

"I did," answered his wife.

"You were at one end of the table and he at the other, I suppose?"

"Yes."

"How did the coffee cup reach him?"

133

"I gave it to the servant, and she placed it before him."

"It passed through no other hands, then?"

"No."

"Who was the servant?"

Mrs. Brenton pondered for a moment.

"I really know very little about her. She had been in our house for a couple of weeks only."

"What was her name?"

"Jane Morton, I think."

"Where is she now, do you know?"

"I do not know."

"She appeared at the inquest, of course?" said Stratton, turning to the sheriff.

"I think she did," was the answer. "I am not sure."

He marked her name down in the note-book.

"How many people were there at the dinner?"

"Including my husband and myself, there were twenty-six."

"Could you give me the name of each of them?"

"Yes, I think so."

She repeated the names, which he took down, with certain notes and comments on each.

"Who sat next your husband at the head of the table?"

"Miss Walker was at his right hand, Mr. Roland at his left."

"Now, forgive me if I ask you if you have ever had any trouble with your husband?"

"Never."

"Never had any quarrel?"

Mrs. Brenton hesitated for a moment.

"No, I don't think we ever had what could be called a quarrel."

"You had no disagreement shortly before the dinner?"

Again Mrs. Brenton hesitated.

"I can hardly call it a disagreement," she said. "We had a little discussion about some of the guests who were to be invited."

"Did he object to any that were there?"

"There was a gentleman there whom he did not particularly like, I think, but he made no objection to his coming; in fact, he seemed to feel that I might imagine he had an objection from a little discussion we had about inviting him; and afterwards, as if to make up for that, he placed this guest at his left hand."

Stratton quickly glanced up the page of his notebook, and marked a little cross before the name of Stephen Roland.

"You had another disagreement with him before, if I might term it so, had you not?"

Mrs. Brenton looked at him surprised.

"What makes you think so?" she said.

"Because you hesitated when I spoke of it."

"Well, we had what you might call a disagreement once at Lucerne, Switzerland."

"Will you tell me what it was about?"

"I would rather not."

"Will you tell me this—was it about a gentleman?"

"Yes," said Mrs. Brenton.

"Was your husband of a jealous disposition?"

"Ordinarily I do not think he was. It seemed to me at the time that he was a little unjust—that's all."

"Was the gentleman in Lucerne?"

"Oh no!"

"In Cincinnati?"

"Yes."

"Was his name Stephen Roland?"

Mrs. Brenton again glanced quickly at the newspaper man, and seemed about to say something, but, checking herself, she simply answered—

"Yes."

Then she leaned back in the armchair and sighed.

"I am very tired," she said. "If it is not absolutely necessary, I prefer not to continue this conversation."

Stratton immediately rose.

"Madam," he said, "I am very much obliged to you for the trouble you have taken to answer my questions, which I am afraid must have seemed impertinent to you, but I assure you that I did not intend them to be so. Now, madam, I would like very much to get a promise from you. I wish that you would promise to see me if I call again, and I, on my part, assure you that unless I have something particularly important to tell you, or to ask, I shall not intrude upon you."

"I shall be pleased to see you at any time, sir."

When the sheriff and the newspaper man reached the other room, the former said—

"Well, what do you think?"

"I think it is an interesting case," was the answer.

"Or, to put it in other words, you think Mrs. Brenton a very interesting lady."

"Officially, sir, you have exactly stated my opinion."

"And I suppose, poor woman, she will furnish an interesting article for the paper?"

"Hang the paper!" said Stratton, with more than his usual vim.

The sheriff laughed. Then he said—

"I confess that to me it seems a very perplexing affair all through. Have you got any light on the subject?"

"My dear sir, I will tell you three important things. First, Mrs. Brenton is innocent. Second, her lawyers are taking the wrong line of defence. Third," tapping his breast-pocket, "I have the name of the murderer in my note-book."

CHAPTER VIII.

"Now," said John Speed to William Brenton, "we have got Stratton fairly started on the track, and I believe that he will ferret out the truth in this matter. But, meanwhile, we must not be idle. You must remember that, with all our facilities for discovery, we really know nothing of the murderer ourselves. I propose we set about this thing just as systematically as Stratton will. The chances are that we shall penetrate the mystery of the whole affair very much quicker than he. As I told you before, I am something of a newspaper man myself; and if, with the facilities of getting into any room in any house, in any city and in any country, and being with a suspected criminal night and day when he never imagines any one is near him—if with all those advantages I cannot discover the real author of that crime before George Stratton does, then I'll never admit that I came from Chicago, or belonged to a newspaper."

"Whom do you think Stratton suspects of the crime? He told the sheriff," said Brenton, "that he had the name in his pocket-book."

"I don't know," said Speed, "but I have my suspicions. You see, he has the names of all the guests at your banquet in that pocket-book of his; but the name of Stephen Roland he has marked with two crosses. The name of the servant he has marked with one cross. Now, I suspect that he believes Stephen Roland committed the crime. You know Roland; what do you think of him?"

"I think he is quite capable of it," answered Brenton, with a frown.

"Still, you are prejudiced against the man," put in Speed, "so your evidence is hardly impartial."

"I am not prejudiced against any one," answered Brenton; "I merely know that man. He is a thoroughly despicable, cowardly character. The only thing that makes me think he would not commit a murder, is that he is too craven to stand the consequences if he were caught. He is a cool villain, but he is a coward. I do not believe he has the courage to commit a crime, even if he thought he would benefit by it."

"Well, there is one thing, Brenton, you can't be accused of flattering a man, and if it is any consolation for you to know, you may be pretty certain that George Stratton is on his track."

"I am sure I wish him success," answered Brenton, gloomily; "if he brings Roland to the gallows I shall not mourn over it."

"That's all right," said Speed; "but now we must be up and doing ourselves. Have you anything to propose?"

"No, I have not, except that we might play the detective on Roland."

"Well, the trouble with that is we would merely be duplicating what Stratton is doing himself. Now, I'll tell you my proposal. Supposing that we consult with Lecocq."

"Who is that? The novelist?"

"Novelist? I don't think he has ever written any novels—not that I remember of."

"Ah, I didn't know. It seemed to me that I remembered his name in connection with some novel."

"Oh, very likely you did. He is the hero of more detective stories than any other man I know of. He was the great French detective."

"What, is he dead, then?"

"Dead? Not a bit of it; he's here with us. Oh, I understand what you mean. Yes, from your point of view, he is dead."

"Where can we find him?"

"Well, I presume, in Paris. He's a first-rate fellow to know, anyhow, and he spends most of his time around his old haunts. In fact, if you want to be certain to find Lecocq, you will generally get him during office hours in the room he used to frequent while in Paris."

"Let us go and see him, then."

"Monsieur Lecocq," said Speed, a moment afterwards, "I wish to introduce to you a new-comer, Mr. Brenton, recently of Cincinnati."

"Ah, my dear Speed," said the Frenchman, "I am very pleased indeed to meet any friend of yours. How is the great Chicago, the second Paris, and how is your circulation?—the greatest in the world, I suppose."

"Well, it is in pretty good order," said Speed; "we circulated from Chicago to Paris here in a very much shorter time than the journey usually occupies down below. Now, can you give us a little of your time? Are you busy just now?"

"My dear Speed, I am always busy. I am like the people of the second Paris. I lose no time, but I have always time to speak with my friends."

"All right," said Speed. "I am like the people of the second Chicago, generally more intent on pleasure than business; but, nevertheless, I have a piece of business for you."

"The second Chicago?" asked Lecocq. "And where is that, pray?"

"Why, Paris, of course," said Speed.

Lecocq laughed.

"You are incorrigible, you Chicagoans. And what is the piece of business?"

"It is the old thing, monsieur. A mystery to be unravelled. Mr. Brenton here wishes to retain you in his case."

"And what is his case?" was the answer.

Lecocq was evidently pleased to have a bit of real work given him.

Speed briefly recited the facts, Brenton correcting him now and then on little points where he was wrong. Speed seemed to think these points immaterial, but Lecocq said that attention to trivialities was the whole secret of the detective business.

"Ah," said Lecocq, sorrowfully, "there is no real trouble in elucidating that mystery. I hoped it would be something difficult; but, you see, with my experience of the old world, and with the privileges one enjoys in this world, things which might be difficult to one below are very easy for us. Now, I shall show you how simple it is."

"Good gracious!" cried Speed, "you don't mean to say you are going to read it right off the reel, like that, when we have been bothering ourselves with it so long, and without success?"

"At the moment," replied the French detective, "I am not prepared to say who committed the deed. That is a matter of detail. Now, let us see what we know, and arrive, from that, at what we do not know. The one fact, of which we are assured on the statement of two physicians from Cincinnati, is that Mr. Brenton was poisoned."

"Well," said Speed, "there are several other facts, too. Another fact is that Mrs. Brenton is accused of the crime."

"Ah! my dear sir," said Lecocq, "that is not pertinent."

"No," said Speed, "I agree with you. I call it very impertinent."

Brenton frowned, at this, and his old dislike to the flippant Chicago man rose to the surface again.

The Frenchman continued marking the points on his long forefinger.

"Now, there are two ways by which that result may have been attained. First, Mr. Brenton may have administered to himself the poison; secondly, the poison may have been administered by some one else."

"Yes," said Speed; "and, thirdly, the poison may have been administered accidentally—you do not seem to take that into account."

"I do not take that into account," calmly replied the Frenchman, "because of its improbability. If there were an accident; if, for instance, the poison was in the sugar, or in some of the viands served, then others than Mr. Brenton would have been poisoned. The fact that one man out of twenty-six was poisoned, and the fact that several people are to benefit by his death, point, it seems to me, to murder; but to be sure of that, I will ask Mr. Brenton one question. My dear sir, did you administer this poison to yourself?"

"Certainly not," answered Brenton.

"Then we have two facts. First, Mr. Brenton was poisoned; secondly, he was poisoned by some person who had an interest in his death. Now we will proceed. When Mr. Brenton sat down to that dinner he was perfectly well. When he arose from that dinner he was feeling ill. He goes to bed. He sees no one but his wife after he has left the dinner-table, and he takes nothing between the time he leaves the dinner-table and the moment he becomes unconscious. Now, that poison must have been administered to Mr. Brenton at the dinner-table. Am I not right?"

"Well, you seem to be," answered Speed.

"Seem? Why, it is as plain as day. There cannot be any mistake."

"All right," said Speed; "go ahead. What next?"

"What next? There were twenty-six people around that table, with two servants to wait on them, making twenty-eight in all. There were twenty-six, I think you said, including Mr. Brenton."

"That is correct."

"Very well. One of those twenty-seven persons has poisoned Mr. Brenton. Do you follow me?"

"We do," answered Speed; "we follow you as closely as you have ever followed a criminal! Go on."

"Very well, so much is clear. These are all facts, not theories. Now, what is the thing that I should do if I were in Cincinnati? I would find out whether one or more of those guests had anything to gain by the death of their host. That done, I would follow the suspected persons. I would have my men find out what each of them had done for a month before the time of the crime. Whoever committed it made some preparation. He did something, too, as you say, in America, to cover up his tracks. Very well. By the keen detective these actions are easily traced. I shall at once place twenty-seven of the best men I know on the track of those twenty-seven persons."

"I call that shadowing with a vengeance," remarked the Chicago man.

"It will be very easy. The one who has committed the crime is certain, when he is alone in his own room, to say something, or to do something, that will show my detective that he is the criminal. So, gentlemen, if you can tell me who those twenty-seven persons are, in three days or a week from this time I will tell you who gave the poison to Mr. Brenton."

"You seem very sure of that," said Speed.

"Sure of it? It is simply child's play. It is mere waiting. If, for instance, at the trial Mrs. Brenton is found guilty, and sentenced, the one who is the guilty party is certain to betray himself or herself as soon as he or she is alone. If it be a man who hopes to marry Mrs. Brenton, he will be overcome with grief at what has happened. He will wring his hands and try to think what can be done to prevent the sentence being carried out. He will argue with himself whether it is better to give himself up and tell the truth, and if he is a coward he will conclude not to do that, but will try to get a pardon, or at least have the capital sentence commuted into life imprisonment. He will possibly be cool and calm in public, but when he enters his own room, when his door is locked, when he believes no one can see him, when he thinks he is alone, then will come his trial. Then his passions and his emotions will betray him. It is mere child's play, as I tell you, and long before there is a verdict I will give you the name of the murderer."

"Very well, then," said Speed, "that is agreed; we will look you up in a week from now."

"I should be pained," said Lecocq, "to put you to that trouble. As soon as I get the report from my men I will communicate with you and let you know the result. In a few days I shall give you the name of the assassin."

"Good-bye, then, until I see you again," answered Speed; and with this he and Brenton took their departure.

"He seems to be very sure of himself," said Brenton.

"He will do what he says, you may depend on that."

The week was not yet up when Monsieur Lecocq met John Speed in Chicago.

"By the look of satisfaction on your face," said Mr. Speed, "I imagine you have succeeded in unravelling the mystery."

"Ah," replied the Frenchman; "if I have the appearance of satisfaction, it is indeed misplaced."

"Then you have not made any discovery?"

"On the contrary, it is all as plain as your big buildings here. It is not for that reason, but because it is so simple that I should be foolish to feel satisfaction regarding it."

"Then who is the person?"

"The assassin," replied the Frenchman, "is one whom no one has seemed to think of, and yet one on whom suspicion should have been the first to fall. The person who did Monsieur Brenton the honour to poison him is none other than the servant girl, Jane Morton."

CHAPTER IX.

"Jane Morton!" cried Speed; "who is she?"

"She is, as you may remember, the girl who carried the coffee from Mrs. Brenton to monsieur."

"And are you sure she is the criminal?"

The great detective did not answer; he merely gave an expressive little French gesture, as though the question was not worth commenting upon.

"Why, what was her motive?" asked Speed.

For the first time in their acquaintance a shade of perplexity seemed to come over the enthusiastic face of the volatile Frenchman.

"You are what you call smart, you Chicago people," he said, "and you have in a moment struck the only point on which we are at a loss."

"My dear sir," returned Speed, "that is the point in the case. Motive is the first thing to look for, it seems to me. You said as much yourself. If you haven't succeeded in finding what motive Jane Morton had for poisoning her employer, it appears to me that very little has been accomplished."

"Ah, you say that before you know the particulars. I am certain we shall find the motive. What I know now is that Jane Morton is the one who put the poison in his cup of coffee."

"It would take a good deal of nerve to do that with twenty-six people around the table. You forget, my dear sir, that she had to pass the whole length of the table, after taking the cup, before giving it to Mr. Brenton."

"Half of the people had their backs to her, and the other half, I can assure you, were not looking at her. If the poison was ready, it was a very easy thing to slip it into a cup of coffee. There was ample time to do it, and that is how it was done."

"May I ask how you arrived at that conclusion?"

"Certainly, certainly, my dear sir. My detectives report that each one of the twenty-seven people they had to follow were shadowed night and day. But only two of them acted suspiciously. These two were Jane Morton and Stephen Roland. Stephen Roland's anxiety is accounted for by the fact that he is evidently in love with Mrs. Brenton. But the change in Jane Morton has been something terrible. She is suffering from the severest pangs of ineffectual remorse. She has not gone out again to service, but occupies a room in one of the poorer quarters of the city—a room that she never leaves except at night. Her whole actions show that she is afraid of the police—afraid of being tracked for her crime. She buys a newspaper every night, locks and bars the door on entering her room, and, with tears streaming from her eyes, reads every word of the criminal news. One night, when she went out to buy her paper, and what food she needed for the next day, she came unexpectedly upon a policeman at the corner. The man was not looking at her at all, nor for her, but she fled, running like a deer, doubling and turning through alleys and back streets until by a very roundabout road she reached her own room. There she locked herself in, and remained without food all next day rather than go out again. She flung herself terror-stricken on the bed, after her room door was bolted, and cried, 'Oh, why did I do it? why did I do it? I shall certainly be found out. If Mrs. Brenton is acquitted, they will be after me next day. I did it to make up to John what he had suffered, and yet if John knew it, he would never speak to me again.'"

"Who is John?" asked Speed.

"Ah, that," said the detective, "I do not know. When we find out who John is, then we shall find the motive for the crime."

"In that case, if I were you, I should try to find John as quickly as possible."

"Yes, my dear sir, that is exactly what should be done, and my detective is now endeavouring to discover the identity of John. He will possibly succeed in a few days. But there is another way of finding out who John is, and perhaps in that you can help me."

"What other way?"

"There is one man who undoubtedly knows who John is, and that is Mr. Brenton. Now, I thought that perhaps you, who know Brenton better than I do, would not mind asking him who John is."

"My dear sir," said Speed, "Brenton is no particular friend of mine, and I only know him well enough to feel that if there is any cross-examination to be done, I should prefer somebody else to do it."

"Why, you are not afraid of him, are you?" asked the detective.

"Afraid of him? Certainly not, but I tell you that Brenton is just a little touchy and apt to take offence. I have found him so on several occasions. Now, as you have practically taken charge of this case, why don't you go and see him?"

"I suppose I shall have to do that," said the Frenchman, "if you will not undertake it."

"No, I will not."

"You have no objection, have you, to going with me?"

"It is better for you to see Brenton alone. I do not think he would care to be cross-examined before witnesses, you know."

"Ah, then, good-bye; I shall find out from Mr. Brenton who John is."

"I am sure I wish you luck," replied Speed, as Lecocq took his departure.

Lecocq found Brenton and Ferris together. The cynical spirit seemed to have been rather sceptical about the accounts given him of the influence that Speed and Brenton, combined, had had upon the Chicago newspaper man. Yet he was interested in the case, and although he still maintained that no practical good would result, even if a channel of communication could be opened between the two states of existence, he had listened with his customary respect to what Brenton had to say.

"Ah," said Brenton, when he saw the Frenchman, "have you any news for me?"

"Yes, I have. I have news that I will exchange, but meanwhile I want some news from you."

"I have none to give you," answered Brenton.

"If you have not, will you undertake to answer any questions I shall ask you, and not take offence if the questions seem to be personal ones?"

"Certainly," said Brenton; "I shall be glad to answer anything as long as it has a bearing on the case."

"Very well, then, it has a very distinct bearing on the case. Do you remember the girl Jane Morton?"

"I remember her, of course, as one of the servants in our employ. I know very little about her, though."

"That is just what I wish to find out. Do you know anything about her?"

"No; she had been in our employ but a fortnight, I think, or perhaps it was a month. My wife attended to these details, of course. I knew the girl was there, that is all."

The Frenchman looked very dubious as Brenton said this, while the latter rather bridled up.

"You evidently do not believe me?" he cried.

Once more the detective gave his customary gesture, and said—

"Ah, pardon me, you are entirely mistaken. I have this to acquaint you with. Jane Morton is the one who murdered you. She did it, she says, partly for the sake of John, whoever he is, and partly out of revenge. Now, of course, you are the only man who can give me information as to the motive. That girl certainly had a motive, and I should like to find out what the motive was."

Brenton meditated for a few moments, and then suddenly brightened up.

"I remember, now, an incident which happened a week of two before

Christmas, which may have a bearing on the case. One night I heard—or thought I heard—a movement downstairs, when I supposed everybody had retired. I took a revolver in my hand, and went cautiously down the stairs. Of course I had no light, because, if there was a burglar, I did not wish to make myself too conspicuous a mark. As I went along the hall leading to the kitchen, I saw there was a light inside; but as soon as they heard me coming the light was put out. When I reached the kitchen, I noticed a man trying to escape through the door that led to the coalshed. I fired at him twice, and he sank to the floor with a groan. I thought I had bagged a burglar sure, but it turned out to be nothing of the kind. He was merely a young man who had been rather late visiting one of the girls. I suspect now the girl he came to see was Jane Morton. As it was, the noise brought the two girls there, and I never investigated the matter or tried to find out which one it was that he had been visiting. They were both terror-stricken, and the young man himself was in a state of great fear. He thought for a moment that he had been killed. However, he was only shot in the leg, and I sent him to the house of a physician who keeps such patients as do not wish to go to the hospital. I did not care to have him go to the hospital, because I was afraid the newspapers would get hold of the incident, and make a sensation of it. The whole thing was accidental; the young fellow realized that, and so, I thought, did the girls; at least, I never noticed anything in their behaviour to show the contrary."

"What sort of a looking girl is Jane Morton?" asked Ferris.

"She is a tall brunette, with snapping black eyes."

"Ah, then, I remember her going into the room where you lay," said Ferris, "on Christmas morning. It struck me when she came out that she was very cool and self-possessed, and not at all surprised."

"All I can say," said Brenton, "is that I never noticed anything in her conduct like resentment at what had happened. I intended to give the young fellow a handsome compensation for his injury, but of course what occurred on Christmas Eve prevented that: I had really forgotten all about the circumstance, or I should have told you of it before."

"Then," said Lecocq, "the thing now is perfectly clear. That black-eyed vixen murdered you out of revenge."

CHAPTER X.

It was evident to George Stratton that he would have no time before the trial came off in which to prove Stephen Roland the guilty person. Besides this, he was in a strange state of mind which he himself could not understand. The moment he sat down to think out a plan by which he could run down the man he was confident had committed the crime, a strange wavering of mind came over him. Something seemed to say to him that he was on the wrong track. This became so persistent that George was bewildered, and seriously questioned his own sanity. Whenever he sat alone in his own room, the doubts arose and a feeling that he was on the wrong scent took possession of him. This feeling became so strong at times that he looked up other clues, and at one time tried to find out the whereabouts of the servant girls who had been employed by the Brentons. Curiously enough, the moment he began this search, his mind seemed to become clearer and easier; and when that happened, the old belief in the guilt of Stephen Roland resumed its sway again. But the instant he tried to follow up what clues he had in that direction, he found himself baffled and assailed again by doubts, and so every effort he put forth appeared to be nullified. This state of mind was so unusual with him that he had serious thoughts of abandoning the whole case and going back to Chicago. He said to himself, "I am in love with this woman and I shall go crazy if I stay here any longer." Then he remembered the trust she appeared to have in his powers of ferreting out the mystery of the case, and this in turn encouraged him and urged him on.

All trace of the girls appeared to be lost. He hesitated to employ a Cincinnati detective, fearing that what he discovered would be given away to the Cincinnati press. Then he accused himself of disloyalty to Mrs. Brenton, in putting his newspaper duty before his duty to her. He was so torn by his conflicting ideas and emotions that at last he resolved to abandon the case altogether and return to Chicago. He packed up his valise and resolved to leave that night for big city, trial or no trial. He had described his symptoms to a prominent physician, and that physician told him that the case was driving him mad, and the best thing he could do was to leave at once for other scenes. He could do no good, and would perhaps end by going insane himself.

As George Stratton was packing his valise in his room, alone, as he thought, the following conversation was taking place beside him.

"It is no use," said Speed; "we are merely muddling him, and not doing any good. The only thing is to leave him alone. If he investigates the Roland part of the case he will soon find out for himself that he is on the wrong track; then he will take the right one."

"Yes," said Brenton; "but the case comes on in a few days. If anything is to be done, it must be done now."

"In that I do not agree with you," said Speed. "Perhaps everything will go all right at the trial, but even if it does not, there is still a certain amount of time. You see how we have spoiled things by interfering. Our first success with him has misled us. We thought we could do anything; we have really done worse than nothing, because all this valuable time has been lost. If he had been allowed to proceed in his own way he would have ferreted out the matter as far as Stephen Roland is concerned, and would have found that there was no cause for his suspicion. As it is he has done nothing. He still believes, if left alone, that Stephen Roland is the criminal. All our efforts to lead him to the residence of Jane Morton have been unavailing. Now, you see, he is on the eve of going back to Chicago."

"Well, then, let him go," said Brenton, despondently.

"With all my heart, say I," answered Speed; "but in any case let us leave him alone."

Before the train started that night Stratton said to himself that he was a new man. Richard was himself again. He was thoroughly convinced of the guilt of Stephen Roland, and wondered why he had allowed his mind to wander off the topic and waste time with other suspicions, for which he now saw there was no real excuse. He had not the time, he felt, to investigate the subject personally, but he flattered himself he knew exactly the man to put on Roland's track, and, instead of going himself to Chicago, he sent off the following despatch:—

"Meet me to-morrow morning, without fail, at the Gibson House. Answer."

Before midnight he had his answer, and next morning he met a man in whom he had the most implicit confidence, and who had, as he said, the rare and valuable gift of keeping his mouth shut.

"You see this portrait?" Stratton said, handing to the other a photograph of Stephen Roland. "Now, I do not know how many hundred chemist shops there are in Cincinnati, but I want you to get a list of them, and you must not omit the most obscure shop in town. I want you to visit every drug store there is in the city, show this photograph to the proprietor and the clerks, and find out if that man bought any chemicals during the week or two preceding Christmas. Find out what drugs he bought, and where he bought them, then bring the information to me."

"How much time do you give me on this, Mr. Stratton?" was the question.

"Whatever time you want. I wish the thing done thoroughly and completely, and, as you know, silence is golden in a case like this."

"Enough said," replied the other, and, buttoning the photograph in his inside pocket, he left the room.

There is no necessity of giving an elaborate report of the trial. Any one who has curiosity in the matter can find the full particulars from the files of any paper in the country. Mrs. Brenton was very pale as she sat in the prisoner's dock, but George Stratton thought he never saw any one look so beautiful. It seemed to him that any man in that crowded courtroom could tell in a moment that she was not guilty of the crime with which she was charged, and he looked at the jury of twelve supposedly good men, and wondered what they thought of it.

The defence claimed that it was not their place to show who committed the murder. That rested with the prosecution. The prosecution, Mr. Benham maintained, had signally failed to do this. However, in order to aid the prosecution, he was quite willing to show how Mr. Brenton came to his death. Then witnesses were called, who, to the astonishment of Mrs. Brenton, testified that her husband had all along had a tendency to insanity. It was proved conclusively that some of his ancestors had died in a lunatic asylum, and one was stated to have committed suicide. The defence produced certain books from Mr. Brenton's library, among them Forbes Winslow's volume on "The Mind and the Brain," to show that Brenton had studied the subject of suicide.

The judge's charge was very colourless. It amounted simply to this: If the jury thought the prosecution had shown Mrs. Brenton to have committed the crime, they were to bring in a verdict of guilty, and if they thought otherwise they were to acquit her; and so the jury retired.

As they left the court-room a certain gloom fell upon all those who were friendly to the fair prisoner.

Despite the great reputation of Benham and Brown, it was the thought of every one present that they had made a very poor defence. The prosecution, on the other hand, had been most ably conducted. It had been shown that Mrs. Brenton was chiefly to profit by her husband's death. The insurance fund alone would add seventy-five thousand dollars to the money she would control. A number of little points that Stratton had given no heed to had been magnified, and appeared then to have a great bearing on the case. For the first time, Stratton admitted to himself that the prosecution had made out a very strong case of circumstantial evidence. The defence, too, had been so deplorably weak that it added really to the strength of the prosecution. A great speech had been expected of Benham, but he did not rise to the occasion, and, as one who knew him said, Benham evidently believed his client guilty.

As the jury retired, every one in the court-room felt that there was little hope for the prisoner; and this feeling was intensified when, a few moments after, the announcement was made in court, just as the judge was preparing to leave the bench, that the jury had agreed on the verdict.

Stratton, in the stillness of the court-room, heard one lawyer whisper to another, "She's doomed."

There was intense silence as the jury slowly filed into their places, and the foreman stood up.

"Gentlemen of the jury," was the question, "have you agreed upon a verdict?"

"We have," answered the foreman.

"Do you find the prisoner guilty or not guilty?"

"Not guilty," was the clear answer.

At this there was first a moment of silence, and then a ripple of applause, promptly checked.

Mrs. Brenton was free.

CHAPTER XI.

George Stratton sat in the court-room for a moment dazed, before he thought of the principal figure in the trial; then he rose to go to her side, but he found that Roland was there before him. He heard her say, "Get me a carriage quickly, and take me away from here."

So Stratton went back to his hotel to meet his Chicago detective. The latter had nothing to report. He told him the number of drug stores he had visited, but all without avail. No one had recognized the portrait.

"All right," said Stratton; "then you will just have to go ahead until you find somebody who does. It is, I believe, only a question of time and perseverance."

Next morning he arose late. He looked over the report of the trial in the morning paper, and then, turning to the leader page, read with rising indignation the following editorial:—

"THE BRENTON CASE.

"The decision of yesterday shows the glorious uncertainty that attends the finding of the average American jury. If such verdicts are to be rendered, we may as well blot out from the statute-book all punishment for all crimes in which the evidence is largely circumstantial. If ever a strong case was made out against a human being it was the case of the prosecution in the recent trial. If ever there was a case in which the defence was deplorably weak, although ably conducted, it was the case that was concluded yesterday. Should we, then, be prepared to say that circumstantial evidence will not be taken by an American jury as ground for the conviction of a murderer? The chances are that, if we draw this conclusion, we shall be entirely wrong. If a man stood in the dock, in the place of the handsome young woman who occupied it yesterday, he would to-day have been undoubtedly convicted of murder. The conclusion, then, to be arrived at seems to be that, unless there is the direct proof of murder against a pretty woman, it is absolutely impossible to get the average jury of men to convict her. It would seem that the sooner we get women on juries, especially where a woman is on trial, the better it will be for the cause of justice."

Then in other parts of the paper there were little items similar to this—

"If Mrs. Brenton did not poison her husband, then who did?"

That afternoon George Stratton paid a visit to Mrs. Brenton. He had hoped she had not seen the paper in question, but he hoped in vain. He found Mrs. Brenton far from elated with her acquittal.

"I would give everything I possess," she said, "to bring the culprit to justice."

After a talk on that momentous question, and when George Stratton held her hand and said good-bye, she asked him—

"When do you go to Chicago?"

"Madam," he said, "I leave for Chicago the moment I find out who poisoned William Brenton."

She answered sadly—

"You may remain a long time in Cincinnati."

"In some respects," said Stratton, "I like Cincinnati better than Chicago."

"You are the first Chicago man I ever heard say that," she replied.

"Ah, that was because they did not know Cincinnati as I do."

"I suppose you must have seen a great deal of the town, but I must confess that from now on I should be very glad if I never saw Cincinnati again. I would like to consult with you," she continued, "about the best way of solving this mystery. I have been thinking of engaging some of the best detectives I can get. I suppose New York would be the place."

"No; Chicago," answered the young man.

"Well, then, that is what I wanted to see you about. I would like to get the very best detectives that can be had. Don't you think that, if they were promised ample reward, and paid well during the time they were working on the case, we might discover the key to this mystery?"

"I do not think much of our detective system," answered Stratton, "although I suppose there is something in it, and sometimes they manage in spite of themselves to stumble on the solution of a crime. Still, I shall be very glad indeed to give you what advice I can on the subject. I may say I have constituted myself a special detective in this case, and that I hope to have the honour of solving the problem."

"You are very good, indeed," she answered, "and I must ask you to let me bear the expense."

"Oh, the paper will do that. I won't be out of pocket at all," said Stratton.

"Well, I hardly know how to put it; but, whether you are successful or not, I feel very grateful to you, and I hope you will not be offended at what I am going to say. Now, promise me that you won't!"

"I shall not be offended," he answered. "It is a little difficult to offend a Chicago newspaper man, you know."

"Now, you mustn't say anything against the newspaper men, for, in spite of the hard things that some of them have said about me, I like them."

"Individually or collectively?"

"I am afraid I must say individually. You said you wouldn't be offended, so after your search is over you must let me——. The labourer is worthy of his hire, or I should say, his reward—you know what I mean. I presume that a young man who earns his living on the daily press is not necessarily wealthy."

"Why, Mrs. Brenton, what strange ideas you have of the world! We newspaper men work at the business merely because we like it. It isn't at all for the money that's in it."

"Then you are not offended at what I have said?"

"Oh, not in the least. I may say, however, that I look for a higher reward than money if I am successful in this search."

"Yes, I am sure you do," answered the lady, innocently. "If you succeed in this, you will be very famous."

"Exactly; it's fame I'm after," said Stratton, shaking her hand once more, and taking his leave.

When he reached his hotel, he found the Chicago detective waiting for him.

"Well, old man," he said, "anything new?"

"Yes, sir. Something very new."

"What have you found out?"

"Everything."

"Very well, let me have it."

"I found out that this man bought, on December 10th, thirty grains of morphia. He had this morphia put up in five-grain capsules. He bought this at the drug store on the corner of Blank Street and Nemo Avenue."

"Good gracious!" answered Stratton. "Then to get morphia he must have had a physician's certificate. Did you find who the physician was that signed the certificate?"

"My dear sir," said the Chicago man, "this person is himself a physician, unless I am very much mistaken. I was told that this was the portrait of Stephen Roland. Am I right?"

"That is the name."

"Well, then, he is a doctor himself. Not doing a very large practice, it is true, but he is a physician. Did you not know that?"

"No," said Stratton; "how stupid I am! I never thought of asking the man's occupation."

"Very well, if that is what you wanted to know, here's the detailed report of my investigation."

When the man left, Stratton rubbed his hands.

"Now, Mr. Stephen Roland, I have you," he said.

CHAPTER XII.

After receiving this information Stratton sat alone in his room and thought deeply over his plans. He did not wish to make a false step, yet there was hardly enough in the evidence he had secured to warrant his giving Stephen Roland up to the police. Besides this, it would put the suspected man at once on his guard, and there was no question but that gentleman had taken every precaution to prevent discovery. After deliberating for a long while, he thought that perhaps the best thing he could do was to endeavour to take Roland by surprise. Meanwhile, before the meditating man stood Brenton and Speed, and between them there was a serious disagreement of opinion.

"I tell you what it is," said Speed, "there is no use in our interfering with Stratton. He is on the wrong track, but, nevertheless, all the influence we can use on him in his present frame of mind will merely do what it did before—it will muddle the man up. Now, I propose that we leave him severely alone. Let him find out his mistake. He will find it out in some way or other, and then he will be in a condition of mind to turn to the case of Jane Morton."

"But don't you see," argued Brenton, "that all the time spent on his present investigation is so much time lost? I will agree to leave him alone, as you say, but let us get somebody else on the Morton case."

"I don't want to do that," said Speed; "because George Stratton has taken a great deal of interest in this search. He has done a great deal now, and I think we should be grateful to him for it."

"Grateful!" growled Brenton; "he has done it from the most purely selfish motives that a man can act upon. He has done it entirely for his paper—for newspaper fame. He has done it for money."

"Now," said Speed, hotly, "you must not talk like that of Stratton to me. I won't say what I think of that kind of language coming from you, but you can see how seriously we interfered with his work before, and how it nearly resulted in his departure for Chicago. I propose now that we leave him alone."

"Leave him alone, then, for any sake," replied Brenton; "I am sure I build nothing on what he can do anyway."

"All right, then," returned Speed, recovering his good nature. "Now, although I am not willing to put any one else on the track of Miss Jane Morton, yet I will tell you what I am willing to do. If you like, we will go to her residence, and influence her to confess her crime. I believe that can be done."

"Very well; I want you to understand that I am perfectly reasonable about the matter. All I want is not to lose any more time."

"Time?" cried Speed; "why, we have got all the time there is. Mrs. Brenton is acquitted. There is no more danger."

"That is perfectly true, I admit; but still you can see the grief under which she labours, because her name is not yet cleared from the odium of the crime. You will excuse me, Speed, if I say that you seem to be working more in the interests of Stratton's journalistic success than in the interests of Mrs. Brenton's good name."

"Well, we won't talk about that," said Speed; "Stratton is amply able to take care of himself, as you will doubtless see. Now, what do you say to our trying whether or not we can influence Jane Morton to do what she ought to do, and confess her crime?"

"It is not a very promising task," replied Brenton; "it is hard to get a person to say words that may lead to the gallows."

"I'm not so sure about that," said Speed; "you know the trouble of mind she is in. I think it more than probable that, after the terror of the last few weeks, it will be a relief for her to give herself up."

"Very well; let us go."

The two men shortly afterwards found themselves in the scantily furnished room occupied by Jane Morton. That poor woman was rocking herself to and fro and moaning over her trouble. Then she suddenly stopped rocking, and looked around the room with vague apprehension in her eyes.

She rose and examined the bolts of the door, and, seeing everything was secure, sat down again.

"I shall never have any peace in this world again," she cried to herself.

She rocked back and forth silently for a few moments.

"I wish," she said, "the police would find out all about it, and then this agony of mind would end."

Again she rocked back and forth, with her hands helplessly in her lap.

"Oh, I cannot do it, I cannot do it!" she sobbed, still rocking to and fro. Finally she started to her feet.

"I will do it," she cried; "I will confess to Mrs. Brenton herself. I will tell her everything. She has gone through trouble herself, and may have mercy on me."

"There, you see," said Speed to Brenton, "we have overcome the difficulty, after all."

"It certainly looks like it," replied Brenton. "Don't you think, however, that we had better stay with her until she does confess? May she not change her mind?"

"Don't let us overdo the thing," suggested Speed; "if she doesn't, come to time, we can easily have another interview with her. The woman's mind is made up. She is in torment, and will be until she confesses her crime. Let us go and leave her alone."

George Stratton was not slow to act when he had once made up his mind. He pinned to the breast of his vest a little shield, on which was the word "detective." This he had often found useful, in a way that is not at all sanctioned by the law, in ferreting out crime in Chicago. As soon as it was evening he paced up and down in front of Roland's house, and on the opposite side of the road. There was a light in the doctor's study, and he thought that perhaps the best way to proceed was to go boldly into the house and put his scheme into operation. However, as he meditated on this, the light was turned low, and in a few moments the door opened. The doctor came down the steps, and out on the pavement, walking briskly along the street. The reporter followed him on the other side of the thoroughfare. Whether to do it in the dark or in the light, was the question that troubled Stratton. If he did it in the dark, he would miss the expression on the face of the surprised man. If he did it in the light, the doctor might recognize him as the Chicago reporter, and would know at once that he was no detective. Still, he felt that if there was anything in his scheme at all, it was surprise; and he remembered the quick gasp of the lawyer Brown when he told him he knew what his defence was. He must be able to note the expression of the man who was guilty of the terrible crime.

Having made up his mind to this, he stepped smartly after the doctor, and, when the latter came under a lamp-post, placed his hand suddenly on his shoulder, and exclaimed—

"Doctor Stephen Roland, I arrest you for the murder of William Brenton!"

CHAPTER XIII.

Stephen Roland turned quietly around and shook the hand from his shoulder. It was evident that he recognized Stratton instantly.

"Is this a Chicago joke?" asked the doctor.

"If it is, Mr. Roland, I think you will find it a very serious one."

"Aren't you afraid that you may find it a serious one?"

"I don't see why I should have any fears in the premises," answered the newspaper man.

"My dear sir, do you not realize that I could knock you down or shoot you dead for what you have done, and be perfectly justified in doing so?"

"If you either knock or shoot," replied the other, "you will have to do it very quickly, for, in the language of the wild and woolly West, I've got the drop on you. In my coat pocket is a cocked revolver with my forefinger on the trigger. If you make a hostile move I can let daylight through you so quickly that you won't know what has struck you."

"Electric light, I think you mean," answered the doctor, quietly. "Even a Chicago man might find it difficult to let daylight through a person at this time in the evening. Now, this sort of thing may be Chicago manners, but I assure you it will not go down here in Cincinnati. You have rendered yourself liable to the law if I cared to make a point of it, but I do not. Come back with me to my study. I would like to talk with you."

Stratton began to feel vaguely that he had made a fool of himself. His scheme had utterly failed. The doctor was a great deal cooler and more collected than he was. Nevertheless, he had a deep distrust of the gentleman, and he kept his revolver handy for fear the other would make a dash to escape him. They walked back without saying a word to each other until they came to the doctor's office. Into the house they entered, and the doctor bolted the door behind them. Stratton suspected that very likely he was walking into a trap, but he thought he would be equal to any emergency that might arise. The doctor walked into the study, and again locked the door of that. Pulling down the blinds, he turned up the gas to its full force and sat down by a table, motioning the newspaper man to a seat on the other side.

"Now," he said calmly to Stratton, "the reason I did not resent your unwarrantable insult is this: You are conscientiously trying to get at the root of this mystery. So am I. Your reason is that you wish to score a victory for your paper. My motive is entirely different, but our object is exactly the same. Now, by some strange combination of circumstances you have come to the conclusion that I committed the crime. Am I right?"

"You are perfectly correct, doctor," replied Stratton.

"Very well, then. Now, I assure you that I am entirely innocent. Of course, I appreciate the fact that this assurance will not in the slightest degree affect your opinion, but I am interested in knowing why you came to your conclusion, and perhaps by putting our heads together, even if I dislike you and you hate me, we may see some light on this matter that has hitherto been hidden. I presume you have no objection at all to co-operate with me?"

"None in the least," was the reply.

"Very well, then. Now, don't mind my feelings at all, but tell me exactly why you have suspected me of being a murderer."

"Well," answered Stratton, "in the first place we must look for a motive. It seems to me that you have a motive for the crime."

"And might I ask what that motive is, or was?"

"You will admit that you disliked Brenton?"

"I will admit that, yes."

"Very well. You will admit also that you were—well, how shall I put it?—let us say, interested in his wife before her marriage?"

"I will admit that; yes."

"You, perhaps, will admit that you are interested in her now?"

"I do not see any necessity for admitting that; but still, for the purpose of getting along with the case, I will admit it. Go on."

"Very good. Here is a motive for the crime, and a very strong one. First, we will presume that you are in love with the wife of the man who is murdered. Secondly, supposing that you are mercenary, quite a considerable amount of money will come to you in case you marry Brenton's widow. Next, some one at that table poisoned him. It was not Mrs. Brenton, who poured out the cup of coffee. The cup of coffee was placed before Brenton, and my opinion is that, until it was placed there, there was no poison in that cup. The doomed man was entirely unsuspicious, and therefore it was very easy for a person to slip enough poison in that cup unseen by anybody at that table, so that when he drank his coffee nothing could have saved him. He rose from the table feeling badly, and he went to his room and died. Now, who could have placed that poison in his cup of coffee? It must have been one of the two that sat at his right and left hand. A young lady sat at his right hand. She certainly did not commit the crime. You, Stephen Roland, sat at his left hand. Do you deny any of the facts I have recited?"

"That is a very ingenious chain of circumstantial evidence. Of course, you do not think it strong enough to convict a man of such a serious crime as murder?"

"No; I quite realize the weakness of the case up to this point. But there is more to follow. Fourteen days before that dinner you purchased at the drug store on the corner of Blank Street and Nemo Avenue thirty grains of morphia. You had the poison put up in capsules of five grains each. What do you say to that bit of evidence added to the circumstantial chain which you say is ingenious?"

The doctor knit his brows and leaned back in his chair.

"By the gods!" he said, "you are right. I did buy that morphia. I remember it now. I don't mind telling you that I had a number of experiments on hand, as every doctor has, and I had those capsules put up at the drug store, but this tragedy coming on made me forget all about the matter."

"Did you take the morphia with you, doctor?"

"No, I did not. And the box of capsules, I do not think, has been opened. But that is easily ascertained."

The doctor rose, went to his cabinet, and unlocked it. From a number of packages he selected a small one, and brought it to the desk, placing it before the reporter.

"There is the package. That contains, as you say, thirty grains of morphia in half a dozen five-grain capsules. You see that it is sealed just as it left the drug store. Now, open it and look for yourself. Here are scales; if you want to see whether a single grain is missing or not, find out for yourself.

"Perhaps," said the newspaper man, "we had better leave this investigation for the proper authorities."

"Then you still believe that I am the murderer of William Brenton?"

"Yes, I still believe that."

"Very well; you may do as you please. I think, however, in justice to myself, you should stay right here, and see that this box is not tampered with until the proper authorities, as you say, come."

Then, placing his hand on the bell, he continued—"Whom shall I send for? An ordinary policeman, or some one from the central office? But, now that I think of it, here is a telephone. We can have any one brought here that you wish. I prefer that neither you nor I leave this room until that functionary has appeared. Name the authority you want brought here," said the doctor, going to the telephone, "and I will have him here if he is in town."

The newspaper man was nonplussed. The Doctor's actions did not seem like those of a guilty man. If he were guilty he certainly had more nerve than any person Stratton had ever met. So he hesitated. Then he said—

"Sit down a moment, doctor, and let us talk this thing over."

"Just as you say," remarked Roland, drawing up his chair again.

Stratton took the package, and looked it over carefully. It was certainly just in the condition in which it had left the drug store; but still, that could have been easily done by the doctor himself.

"Suppose we open this package?" he said to Roland.

"With all my heart," said the doctor, "go ahead;" and he shoved over to him a little penknife that was on the table.

The reporter took the package, ran the knife around the edge, and opened it. There lay six capsules, filled, as the doctor had said. Roland picked up one of them, and looked at it critically.

"I assure you," he said, "although I am quite aware you do not believe a word I say, that I have not seen those capsules before."

He drew towards him a piece of paper, opened the capsule, and, let the white powder fall on the paper. He looked critically at the powder, and a shade of astonishment came over his face. He picked up the penknife, took a particle on the tip of it, and touched it with his tongue.

"Don't fool with that thing!" said Stratton.

"Oh, my dear fellow," he said, "morphia is not a poison in small quantities."

The moment he had tasted it, however, he suddenly picked up the paper, put the five grains on his tongue, and swallowed them.

Instantly the reporter sprang to his feet. He saw at once the reason for all the assumed coolness. The doctor was merely gaining time in order to commit suicide.

"What have you done?" cried the reporter.

"Done, my dear fellow? nothing very much. This is not morphia; it is sulphate of quinine."

CHAPTER XIV.

In the morning Jane Morton prepared to meet Mrs. Brenton, and make her confession. She called at the Brenton residence, but found it closed, as it had been ever since the tragedy of Christmas morning. It took her some time to discover the whereabouts of Mrs. Brenton, who, since the murder, had resided with a friend except while under arrest.

For a moment Mrs. Brenton did not recognize the thin and pale woman who stood before her in a state of such extreme nervous agitation, that it seemed as if at any moment she might break down and cry.

"I don't suppose you'll remember me, ma'am," began the girl, "but I worked for you two weeks before—before——"

"Oh yes," said Mrs. Brenton, "I remember you now. Have you been ill? You look quite worn and pale, and very different from what you did the last time I saw you."

"Yes," said the girl, "I believe I have been ill.".

"You believe; aren't you sure?"

"I have been very ill in mind, and troubled, and that is the reason I look so badly,—Oh, Mrs. Brenton, I wanted to tell you of something that has been weighing on my mind ever since that awful day! I know you can never forgive me, but I must tell it to you, or I shall go crazy."

"Sit down, sit down," said the lady, kindly; "you know what trouble I have been in myself. I am sure that I am more able to sympathize now with one who is in trouble than ever I was before."

"Yes, ma'am; but you were innocent, and I am guilty. That makes all the difference in the world."

"Guilty!" cried Mrs. Brenton, a strange fear coming over her as she stared at the girl; "guilty of what?"

"Oh, madam, let me tell you all about it. There is, of course, no excuse; but I'll begin at the beginning. You remember a while before Christmas that John came to see me one night, and we sat up very late in the kitchen, and your husband came down quietly, and when we heard him coming we put out the light and just as John was trying to get away, your husband shot twice at him, and hit him the second time?"

"Oh yes," said Mrs. Brenton, "I remember that very well. I had forgotten about it in my own trouble; but I know that my husband intended to do something for the young man. I hope he was not seriously hurt?"

"No, ma'am; he is able to be about again now as well as ever, and is not even lame, which we expected he would be. But at the time I thought he was going to be lame all the rest of his life, and perhaps that is the reason I did what I did. When everything was in confusion in the house, and it was certain that we would all have to leave, I did a very wicked thing. I went to your room, and I stole some of your rings, and some money that was there, as well as a lot of other things that were in the room. It seemed to me then, although, of course, I know now how wicked it was, that you owed John something for what he had gone through, and I thought that he was to be lame, and that you would never miss the things; but, oh! madam, I have not slept a night since I took them. I have been afraid of the police and afraid of being found out. I have pawned nothing, and they are all just as I took them, and I have brought them back here to you, with every penny of the money. I know you can never forgive me, but I am willing now to be given up to the police, and I feel better in my mind than I have done ever since I took the things."

"My poor child!" said Mrs. Brenton, sympathetically, "was that all?"

"All?" cried the girl. "Yes, I have brought everything back."

"Oh, I don't mean that, but I am sorry you have been worried over anything so trivial. I can see how at such a time, and feeling that you had been wronged, a temptation to take the things came to you. But I hope you will not trouble any more about the matter. I will see that John is compensated for all the injury he received, as far as it is possible for money to compensate him. I hope you will keep the money. The other things, of course, I shall take back, and I am glad you came to tell me of it before telling any one else. I think, perhaps, it is better never to say anything to anybody about this. People might not understand just what temptation you were put to, and they would not know the circumstances of the case, because nobody knows, I think, that John was hurt. Now, my dear girl, do not cry. It is all right. Of course you never will touch anything again that does not belong to you, and the suffering you have gone through has more than made up for all the wrong you have done. I am sure that I forgive you quite freely for it, and I think it was very noble of you to come and tell me about it."

Mrs. Brenton took the package from the hands of the weeping girl, and opened it. She found everything there, as the girl had said. She took the money and offered it to Jane Morton. The girl shook her head.

"No," she cried, "I cannot touch it. I cannot, indeed. It has been enough misery to me already."

"Very well," said Mrs. Brenton. "I would like very much to see John. Will you bring him to me?"

The girl looked at her with startled eyes.

"You will not tell him?" she said.

"No indeed, I shall tell him nothing. But I want to do what I can for him as I said. I suppose you are engaged to be married?"

"Yes," answered the girl; "but if he knew of this he never, never would marry me."

"If he did not," said Mrs. Brenton, "he would not be worthy of you. But he shall know nothing about it. You will promise to come here and see me with him, will you not?"

"Yes, madam," said the girl.

"Then good-bye, until I see you again."

Mrs. Brenton sat for a long time thinking over this confession. It took her some time to recover her usual self-possession, because for a moment she had thought the girl was going to confess that she committed murder. In comparison with that awful crime, the theft seemed so trivial that Mrs. Brenton almost smiled when she thought of the girl's distress.

"Well," said John Speed to Mr. Brenton, "if that doesn't beat the Old Harry. Now I, for one, am very glad of it, if we come to the real truth of the matter."

"I am glad also," said Brenton, "that the girl is not guilty, although I must say things looked decidedly against her."

"I will tell you why I am glad," said Speed. "I am glad because it will take some of the superfluous conceit out of that French detective Lecocq. He was so awfully sure of himself. He couldn't possibly be mistaken. Now, think of the mistakes that man must have made while he was on earth, and had the power which was given into his hands in Paris. After all, Stratton is on the right track, and he will yet land your friend Roland in prison. Let us go and find Lecocq. This is too good to keep."

"My dear sir," said Brenton, "you seem to be more elated because of your friend Stratton than for any other reason. Don't you want the matter ferreted out at all?"

"Why, certainly I do; but I don't want it ferreted out by bringing an innocent person into trouble."

"And may not Stephen Roland be an innocent person?"

"Oh, I suppose so; but I do not think he is."

"Why do you not think so?"

"Well, if you want the real reason, simply because George Stratton thinks he isn't. I pin my faith to Stratton."

"I think you overrate your friend Stratton."

"Overrate him, sir? That is impossible. I love him so well that I hope he will solve this mystery himself, unaided and alone, and that in going back to Chicago he will be smashed to pieces in a railway accident, so that we can have him here to congratulate him."

CHAPTER XV.

"I suppose," said Roland, "you thought for a moment I was trying to commit suicide. I think, Mr. Stratton, you will have a better opinion of me by-and-by. I shouldn't be at all surprised if you imagined I induced you to come in here to get you into a trap."

"You are perfectly correct," said Stratton; "and I may say, although that was my belief, I was not in the least afraid of you, for I had you covered all the time."

"Well," remarked Roland, carelessly, "I don't want to interfere with your business at all, but I wish you wouldn't cover me quite so much; that revolver of yours might go off."

"Do you mean to say," said Stratton, "that there is nothing but quinine in those capsules?"

"I'll tell you in a moment," as he opened them one by one. "No, there is nothing but quinine here. Thirty grains put up in five-grain capsules."

George Stratton's eyes began to open. Then he slowly rose, and looked with horrified face at the doctor.

"My God!" he cried; "who got the thirty grains of morphia?"

"What do you mean?" asked the doctor.

"Mean? Why, don't you see it? It is a chemist's mistake. Thirty grains of quinine have been sent you. Thirty grains of morphia have been sent to somebody else. Was it to William Brenton?"

"By Jove!" said the doctor, "there's something in that. Say, let us go to the drug store."

The two went out together, and walked to the drug store on the corner of Blank Street and Nemo Avenue.

"Do you know this writing?" said Doctor Roland to the druggist, pointing to the label on the box.

"Yes," answered the druggist; "that was written by one of my assistants."

"Can we see him for a few moments?"

"I don't know where he is to be found. He is a worthless fellow, and has gone to the devil this last few weeks with a rapidity that is something startling."

"When did he leave?"

"Well, he got drunk and stayed drunk during the holidays, and I had to discharge him. He was a very valuable man when he was sober; but he began to be so erratic in his habits that I was afraid he would make a ghastly mistake some time, so I discharged him before it was too late."

"Are you sure you discharged him before it was too late?"

The druggist looked at the doctor, whom he knew well, and said, "I never heard of any mistake, if he did make it."

"You keep a book, of course, of all the prescriptions sent out?"

"Certainly."

"May we look at that book?"

"I shall be very glad to show it to you. What month or week?"

"I want to see what time you sent this box of morphia to me."

"You don't know about what time it was, do you?

"Yes; it must have been about two weeks before Christmas."

The chemist looked over the pages of the book, and finally said, "Here it is."

"Will you let me look at that page?"

"Certainly."

The doctor ran his finger down the column, and came to an entry written in the same hand.

"Look here," he said to Stratton, "thirty grains of quinine sent to William Brenton, and next to it thirty grains of morphia sent to Stephen Roland. I see how it was. Those prescriptions were mixed up. My package went to poor Brenton."

The druggist turned pale.

"I hope," he said, "nothing public will come of this."

"My dear sir," said Roland, "something public will have to come of it. You will oblige me by ringing up the central police station, as this book must be given in charge of the authorities."

"Look here," put in Stratton, his newspaper instinct coming uppermost, "I want to get this thing exclusively for the Argus."

"Oh, I guess there will be no trouble about that. Nothing will be made public until to-morrow, and you can telegraph to-night if we find the box of capsules in Brenton's residence. We must take an officer with us for that purpose, but you can caution or bribe him to keep quiet until to-morrow."

When the three went to William Brenton's residence they began a search of the room in which Brenton had died, but nothing was found. In the closet of the room hung the clothes of Brenton, and going through them Stratton found in the vest pocket of one of the suits a small box containing what was described as five-grain capsules of sulphate of quinine. The doctor tore one of these capsules apart, so as to see what was in it. Without a moment's hesitation he said—

"There you are! That is the morphia. There were six capsules in this box, and one of them is missing. William Brenton poisoned himself! Feeling ill, he doubtless took what he thought was a dose of quinine. Many men indulge in what we call the quinine habit. It is getting to be a mild form of tippling. Brenton committed unconscious suicide!"

CHAPTER XVI.

A group of men; who were really alive, but invisible to the searchers, stood in the room where the discovery was made. Two of the number were evidently angry, one in one way and one in another. The rest of the group appeared to be very merry. One angry man was Brenton himself, who was sullenly enraged. The other was the Frenchman, Lecocq, who was as deeply angered as Brenton, but, instead of being sullen, was exceedingly voluble.

"I tell you," he cried, "it is not a mistake of mine. I went on correct principles from the first. I was misled by one who should have known better. You will remember, gentlemen," he continued, turning first to one and then the other, "that what I said was that we had certain facts to go on. One of those facts I got from Mr. Brenton. I said to him in your presence, 'Did you poison yourself?' He answered me, as I can prove by all of you, 'No, I did not.' I took that for a fact. I thought I was speaking to a reasonable man who knew what he was talking about."

"Haven't I told you time and again," answered Brenton, indignantly, "that it was a mistake? You asked me if I poisoned myself. I answered you that I did not. Your question related to suicide. I did not commit suicide. I was the victim of a druggist's mistake. If you had asked me if I had taken medicine before I went to bed, I should have told you frankly, 'Yes. I took one capsule of quinine.' It has been my habit for years, when I feel badly. I thought nothing of that."

"My dear sir," said Lecocq, "I warned you, and I warned these gentlemen, that the very things that seem trivial to a thoughtless person are the things that sometimes count. You should have told me everything. If you took anything at all, you should have said so. If you had said to me, 'Monsieur Lecocq, before I retired I took five grains of quinine,' I should have at once said; 'Find where that quinine is, and see if it is quinine, and see if there has not been a mistake.' I was entirely misled; I was stupidly misled."

"Well, if there was stupidity," returned Brenton, "it was your own."

"Come, come, gentlemen," laughed Speed, "all's well that ends well.

Everybody has been mistaken, that's all about it. The best detective minds of Europe and America, of the world, and of the spirit-land, have been misled. You are all wrong. Admit it, and let it end."

"My dear sir," said Lecocq, "I shall not admit anything. I was not wrong; I was misled. It was this way——"

"Oh, now, for goodness' sake don't go over it all again. We understand the circumstances well enough."

"I tell you," cried Brenton, in an angry tone, "that——

"Come, come," said Speed, "we have had enough of this discussion. I tell you that you are all wrong, every one of you. Come with me, Brenton, and we will leave this amusing crowd."

"I shall do nothing of the kind," answered Brenton, shortly.

"Oh, very well then, do as you please. I am glad the thing is ended, and I am glad it is ended by my Chicago friend."

"Your Chicago friend!" sneered Brenton, slightingly; "It was discovered by Doctor Stephen Roland."

"My dear fellow," said Speed, "Stephen Roland had all his time to discover the thing, and didn't do it, and never would have done it, if George Stratton hadn't encountered him. Well, good-bye, gentlemen; I am sorry to say that I have had quite enough of this discussion. But one thing looms up above it all, and that is that Chicago is ahead of the world in everything—in detection as well as in fires."

"My dear sir," cried Lecocq, "it is not true. I will show you in a moment—"

"You won't show me," said Speed, and he straightway disappeared.

"Come, Ferris," said Brenton, "after all, you are the only friend I seem to have; come with me."

"Where are you going?" asked Ferris, as they left.

"I want to see how my wife takes the news."

"Don't," said Mr. Ferris—"don't do anything of the kind. Leave matters just where they are. Everything has turned out what you would call all right. You see that your interference, as far as it went, was perfectly futile and useless. I want now to draw your attention to other things."

"Very well, I will listen to you," said Brenton, "if you come with me and see how my wife takes the news. I want to enjoy for even a moment or two her relief and pleasure at finding that her good name is clear."

"Very well," assented Ferris, "I will go with you."

When they arrived they found the Chicago reporter ahead of them. He had evidently told Mrs. Brenton all the news, and her face flushed with eager pleasure as she listened to the recital.

"Now," said the Chicago man, "I am going to leave Cincinnati. Are you sorry I am going?"

"No," said Mrs. Brenton, looking him in the face, "I am not sorry."

Stratton flushed at this, and then said, taking his hat in his hand, "Very well, madam, I shall bid you good day."

"I am not sorry," said Mrs. Brenton, holding out her hand, "because I am going to leave Cincinnati myself, and I hope never to see the city again. So if you stayed here, you see, I should never meet you again, Mr. Stratton."

"Alice," cried Stratton, impulsively grasping her hand in both of his, "don't you think you would like Chicago as a place of residence?"

"George," she answered, "I do not know. I am going to Europe, and shall be there for a year or two."

Then he said eagerly—

"When you return, or if I go over there to see you after a year or two, may I ask you that question again?"

"Yes," was the whispered answer.

"Come," said Brenton to Ferris, "let us go."

About Author

Robert Barr (16 September 1849 – 21 October 1912) was a Scottish-Canadian short story writer and novelist.

Early years in Canada

Robert Barr was born in Barony, Lanark, Scotland to Robert Barr and Jane Watson. In 1854, he emigrated with his parents to Upper Canada at the age of four years old. His family settled on a farm near the village of Muirkirk. Barr assisted his father with his job as a carpenter, and developed a sound work ethic. Robert Barr then worked as a steel smelter for a number of years before he was educated at Toronto Normal School in 1873 to train as a teacher.

After graduating Toronto Normal School, Barr became a teacher, and eventually headmaster/principal of the Central School of Windsor, Ontario in 1874. While Barr worked as head master of the Central School of Windsor, Ontario, he began to contribute short stories—often based on personal experiences, and recorded his work. On August 1876, when he was 27, Robert Barr married Ontario-born Eva Bennett, who was 21. According to the 1891 England Census, the couple appears to have had three children, Laura, William, and Andrew.

In 1876, Barr quit his teaching position to become a staff member of publication, and later on became the news editor for the Detroit Free Press. Barr wrote for this newspaper under the pseudonym, "Luke Sharp." The idea for this pseudonym was inspired during his morning commute to work when Barr saw a sign that read "Luke Sharp, Undertaker." In 1881, Barr left Canada to return to England in order to start a new weekly version of "The Detroit Free Press Magazine."

London years

In 1881 Barr decided to "vamoose the ranch", as he called the process of immigration in search of literary fame outside of Canada, and relocated to London to continue to write/establish the weekly English edition of the Detroit Free Press. During the 1890s, he broadened his literary works, and started writing novels from the popular crime genre. In 1892 he founded the magazine The Idler, choosing Jerome K. Jerome as his collaborator (wanting, as Jerome said, "a popular name"). He retired from its co-editorship in 1895.

In London of the 1890s Barr became a more prolific author—publishing a book a year—and was familiar with many of the best-selling authors of his day, including :Arnold Bennett, Horatio Gilbert Parker, Joseph Conrad, Bret Harte, Rudyard Kipling, H. Rider Haggard, H. G. Wells, and George Robert Gissing. Barr was well-spoken, well-cultured due to travel, and considered a "socializer."

Because most of Barr's literary output was of the crime genre, his works were highly in vogue. As Sherlock Holmes stories were becoming well-known, Barr wrote and published in the Idler the first Holmes parody, "The Adventures of "Sherlaw Kombs" (1892), a spoof that was continued a decade later in another Barr story, "The Adventure of the Second Swag" (1904). Despite those jibes at the growing Holmes phenomenon, Barr remained on very good terms with its creator Arthur Conan Doyle. In Memories and Adventures, a serial memoir published 1923–24, Doyle described him as "a volcanic Anglo—or rather Scot-American, with a violent manner, a wealth of strong adjectives, and one of the kindest natures underneath it all".

In 1904, Robert Barr completed an unfinished novel for Methuen & Co. by the recently deceased American author Stephen Crane entitled The O'Ruddy, a romance.Despite his reservations at taking on the project, Barr reluctantly finished the last eight chapters due to his longstanding friendship with Crane and his common-law wife, Cora, the war correspondent and bordello owner.

Death

The 1911 census places Robert Barr, "a writer of fiction," at Hillhead, Woldingham, Surrey, a small village southeast of London, living with his wife, Eva, their son William, and two female servants. At this home, the author died from heart disease on 21 October 1912.

Writing Style

Barr's volumes of short stories were often written with an ironic twist in the story with a witty, appealing narrator telling the story. Barr's other works also include numerous fiction and non-fiction contributions to periodicals. A few of his mystery stories and stories of the supernatural were put in anthologies, and a few novels have been republished. His writings have also attracted scholarly attention. His narrative personae also featured moral and editorial interpolations within their tales. Barr's achievements were recognized by an honorary degree from the University of Michigan in 1900.

His protagonists were journalists, princes, detectives, deserving commercial and social climbers, financiers, the new woman of bright wit and aggressive accomplishment, and lords. Often, his characters were stereotypical and romanticized.

Barr wrote fiction in an episode-like format. He developed this style when working as an editor for the newspaper Detroit Press. Barr developed his skill with the anecdote and vignette; often only the central character serves to link the nearly self-contained chapters of the novels. (Source: Wikipedia)

NOTABLE WORKS

In a Steamer Chair and Other Stories (Thirteen short stories by one of the most famous writers in his day -1892)

"The Face And The Mask" (1894) consists of twenty-four delightful short stories.

In the Midst of Alarms (1894, 1900, 1912), a story of the attempted Fenian invasion of Canada in 1866.

From Whose Bourne (1896) Novel in which the main character, William Brenton, searches for truth to set his wife free.

One Day's Courtship (1896)

Revenge! (Collection of 20 short stories, Alfred Hitchcock-like style, thriller with a surprise ending)

The Strong Arm

A Woman Intervenes (1896), a story of love, finance, and American journalism.

Tekla: A Romance of Love and War (1898)

Jennie Baxter, Journalist (1899)

The Unchanging East (1900)

The Victors (1901)

A Prince of Good Fellows (1902)

Over The Border: A Romance (1903)

The O'Ruddy, A Romance, with Stephen Crane (1903)

A Chicago Princess (1904)

The Speculations of John Steele (1905)

The Tempestuous Petticoat (1905–12)

A Rock in the Baltic (1906)

The Triumphs of Eugène Valmont (1906)

The Measure of the Rule (1907)

Stranleigh's Millions (1909)

The Sword Maker (Medieval action/adventure novel, genre: Historical Fiction-1910)

The Palace of Logs (1912)

"The Ambassadors Pigeons" (1899)

"And the Rigor of the Game" (1892)

"Converted" (1896)

"Count Conrad's Courtship" (1896)

"The Count's Apology" (1896)

"A Deal on Change " (1896)

"The Exposure of Lord Stanford" (1896)

"Gentlemen: The King!"

"The Hour-Glass" (1899)

"An invitation" (1892)

" A Ladies Man"

"The Long Ladder" (1899)

"Mrs. Tremain" (1892)

" Transformation" (1896)

"The Understudy" (1896)

" The Vengeance of the Dead" (1896)

"The Bromley Gibbert's Story" (1896)

" Out of Thun" (1896)

"The Shadow of Greenback" (1896)

"Flight of the Red Dog" (fiction)

"Lord Stranleigh Abroad" (1913)

"One Day's Courtship and the Herald's of Fame" (1896)

"Cardillac"

"Dr. Barr's Tales"

"The Triumphs of Eugene Valmont"